Lina R. Breitkreutz

THE NEW FAVOURITE

Lina R. Breitkreutz

THE NEW FAVOURITE

Author: Lina R. Breitkreutz

Text editor: Anikó Konrádné Tamás

Translated by: Judit Gabris

Original title: Az új kedvenc

Cover: Balázs Németh

Typesetting: Zoltán Szabó (pixelfaragok.hu)

Acknowledgements

Thanks to my daughter for believing in me. I love you, berry head.

Special thanks to my partner; without him I wouldn't be who I am today.

To Enikő, without whom the protagonist would be an alcoholic writer.

To Anikó for editing. Without them my manuscript would not even have made it to the publisher.

To Kriszti, for the Chapter of the Sixth Orphan. I'm looking forward to reading your book very much!

Thanks to the owner of the Black Castle of Balatonederics, without whose neglect I would not have noticed this crumbling beauty.

Table of Contents

CHAPTER 1

THE OLD MAN

JUNE 8, 1841, EDERICS, HUNGARY

The distinguished ambassador has arrived. He got out of the car and immediately hurried to the lady of the house. He had an imposing, heavy, deep-voiced, commanding presence. Beyond his noble rank and his political office, it was his moral integrity, wisdom, and truthfulness that had earned him the respect of an entire country. He was a gentleman through and through. The wise man of his homeland.

He had come to attend the funeral of a friend and relative; the occasion was even more of a tragedy to him because of her five orphaned children. His integrity and commitment to his family demanded that he give even greater support to his niece Emma at this time.

"Uncle Francis! Thank you for coming," Emma whispered, burying her face in his shoulder after their long embrace.

"Of course I did, Emma. This is a terrible blow to our family," the old man said in a soothing tone.

"What are we going to do now?" She looked at her five orphans, and burst out sobbing.

"I'll help you with whatever I can. As long as I live, you will want for nothing, and neither will the children. I'll stay as long as I can, Emma."

Not even the heat of the summer sun could comfort the family or the dwellers of the estate. The entire county was mourning the loss of the distinguished chief justice Louis Nedeczky.

Chapter 2

The new favourite

2018, Balatonederics, Hungary

Paul was in the middle of storytelling when I glimpsed at the tower-like turret of a building. From this little detail I realized that it was part of a castle. I couldn't make out any more from the speeding car as the land all around was densely overgrown with wild thicket. I looked at Paul and blurted out:

"It's a castle! This is a castle! Let's stop here! Turn around! Let's go back! Let's check it out! I want to have a look at it! And you love old castles too!"

"Okay, okay, relax! I can't turn around here, wait a bit! "

"Here's the next village, turn around here!" I snapped again.

"Seriously?" You don't say! I see it too."

Paul smiled at how I could be just a derelict ruin away from breathless euphoria. Especially when that ruin is a castle. Then I may even enter a full-blown frenzy!

We turned around where the road widened a little, and now I was rubbernecking out of the window to catch as much detail as possible.

The place was surrounded by fields of varying shapes on both sides and to the rear. At the entrance, the main road curtailed the enormous jungle. To the right of the plot, I saw a dirt road with tracks left by tractors.

"That's it. Turn right here! We can go in here!"

"All right, all right..." my beloved cooed, smiling. "Relax, we'll go in".

The weather was grey, cold, and wintry. The unkempt garden a memento to the withering of nature in autumn with the lifeless husks of trees and bushes all around. We're in the right place, I thought. Grab the phone, we must make a record of this!

As we turned onto the dirt road, we were able to drive 5-10 meters further down. The small path evinced signs of other visitors to the place too.

The sight before my eyes struck me as wonderful, sad, scary and fascinating at the same time. It was indeed a castle. Some patches of plaster still clung to the walls, so my imagination quickly recovered the original shape of the building. In the middle, where a gate would have stood and served as a main entrance, a startlingly deep black hole, lined with bare bricks gaped. We advanced past it into a foreboding, dingy space that made the ruin appear to try to swallow us.

With each step, we struggled with the dense overgrowth to get inside. The base of the building was surrounded by fallen plaster and a web of green creepers covering it. The whole building looked bloodcurdling ghoulish and eerie. Perhaps it was the wintry, overcast weather, and the lifeless thicket that was waiting for spring to be reborn.

The ground-floor windows, some of them just empty frames, or mere howling gaps in the brickwork, peered through their rusty bars. In the eastern corner of the building, the window was completely obscured by the creepers on the wall. The edges of the stairs to the main entrance were still visible from the settled rubble. I went up through the main entrance and stepped into the building. A fabulous but fragmented, dusty mosaic greeted me on the ground. A white horse with his rider, who is talking to the hunter in front of him. How gorgeous this must have been once, I thought to myself.

My eyes began to adjust to the darkness. Looking left and right, I saw the mysterious corridor which was also murky. It stretched into a frameless door at each end where I could only discern blackness. "Well, we're not going that way, that's for sure!" I shivered at the thought. "Who knows what may fall on me, what I might tread on, or what animal could attack me in the dark?" Paul did not brave the dangers of the tumbledown ruin and waited outside. But I went inside, to the stairwell in the middle of the building and started going up the stairs.

I could also admire a second beautiful mosaic on the ground at the turn of the stairs. As I looked up, I noticed that the handrail to the upstairs landing was missing. My heart missed a beat. In my imagination, this is a fantastic building with an impressive, spacious interior. I saw a beautiful staircase in front of me. Stuccos on walls, ceilings, and all the furniture of the era was in its place in my mind's eye. The colors, spaces and furnishings were in perfect accord. In reality, I though this beauty is a desolate ruin that only the wind whistles through. I didn't even count the rooms, I was so busy getting out. Each winding hallway, then room, led to the next. At first, it seemed to go on infinitely and be much bigger than I had estimated from the outside.

It was a distressing sight. Why did the owner allow time to destroy this beauty? Why don't they see what I see? Apart from the crumbling plaster and a few scrawls on the walls, there was nothing to see, so I came out.

Still eager to take in more, Paul and I walked around the outside of the building. To the rear, the garden was slightly more accessible. The color of this side of the building was of dirty cherries; the castle had a long staircase in the middle. I went up cautiously, but found only a zig-zag branch leading into the darkness lined with cobwebs and dried husks of creepers. The style of the tiles that had fallen here and there harked back to the '80s. It was probably the last time the building was used.

"It looks scary and depressing from here," I said to Paul, then turned pensively and headed down the stairs. I thought to hold onto the handrail on my way down, but halfway down the rail abruptly vanished.

"Who might own this building?" Paul asked with a bit of excitement in his voice due to the state of the ruin.

"I haven't a clue. Such a pity that the owner let it go to pot," I said. "I want this castle!"

"Oh, of course you do," Paul laughed. "Do you know what it would cost to fix this up? Five apartments like ours wouldn't be enough. And then it must be maintained. Just because we live well, we don't have to buy a castle just yet. Besides, what would we do in such a large house? This is too big for us to live in. Or should we move in half the village too?"

"Don't spoil my dreams, honey," I said bitterly.

"Bah!" he quipped. "We can go now. I think I've seen everything".

For the rest of our New Year's vacation, I couldn't think of anything else in my spare time than the derelict castle. It had become the new favorite out of many. The conviction began to grow in me: I wanted this castle for myself! I needed this!

THE AIRPORT

After our year-end getaway, we eased ourselves back into our workaday lives. I kept my feet on the ground, and, aside from daydreaming about my new favorite, our days passed uneventfully.

Being German, Paul started planning our annual holidays and smaller holiday breaks in January – unfathomably early for me. As for me, I bought new vegetable seeds for my future seedlings on the balcony. I love watching the cycles of nature as a life waxes and wanes in plants. I can see when they are strong, when the weaker seedlings are about to die, or when they finally bear fruit and stand proudly in their pots, weighed down by their tomatoes. They produce beautiful, healthy vegetables, then complete their life cycle and die, as they are meant to.

In the evenings, before going to bed, I flicked through the photos of the castle. My imagination, far from peacefully letting the memories be, began to stir more and more fervently. One moment after another: "What color should I make the new windows? Could the walls on the outside stay ocher-pale yellow, as it behooves a castle? Which part of it would we make into the bedroom? Ah, now I'm kicking myself that I didn't go around the house. But it was so overwhelming…"

"Look, sweetheart," I showed Paul one of the pictures, "there was an indent in the wall on the side of the house. Maybe there was a statue there a long time ago."

"Yes, it is possible," he replied flatly, then went on burying himself in one of his newly acquired history books. It's amazing how out of it he can be in the evenings. His blondish mousy hair with his receding hairline and long sideburns make his already long face seem even longer. It doesn't do him any favors, but his blue eyes make up for everything.

I rolled myself back under my blanket and immersed myself in my boundless fantasies. I imagined making my first visit to the estate, now as an owner. Then another image appeared of me talking to the head of the renovation project about the details of the castle. Then, one of me discussing how to arrange the garden with the gardener. A thousand and one details ricocheted around my mind, and the mounting excitement kept fueling my impossible dream: I want this house! The next moment, my saner half piped up: "Whatever for?", intimating frustration; and this is where my feverish planning came to a halt.

*

We were chugging through our days when I got a call to go to California.

The publisher there was working to make my book a success. They are on top of things in marketing. I set off to them and, of course, to a friend of mine who lived more than ten thousand miles away, yet remained a close friend.

While waiting at the airport, I thought I'd search the internet for the castle to see if I could find a description of it. "Lina, you're getting obsessed," I murmured to myself, jokingly. "Well, let's see; search engine: place name plus word: castle." Thousands of hits, as we have come to expect. Wide-eyed, I read the headlines: Black Castle, Ghost Castle, Cursed Castle. "What the hell? That's definitely not what we saw." I clicked on the first hit. It was a site cataloging historic buildings with many pictures detailing their condition. It was the one! The story of the house's inhabitants, in a nutshell: every owner had committed suicide. Oh! And the cook was murdered. "Oh my goodness. A real haunted castle! Is there such a thing in Hungary?" I intoned sarcastically as I tugged my eyebrows left and right. My earnest research efforts were suddenly interrupted by the sound of the crashing crowd about to check in.

*

It was a long and uneventful flight. Including a Frankfurt transfer, over 12 hours in the air. Plus the packing at home, going to the airport, waiting at the gates, then getting out of the airport to the hotel, a chaos of voices and loads of people. This palaver is not for me. The San Francisco airport staff searched me carefully, I must look like a regular terrorist for sure. I got out of the crowd after quick cross-examining. Chongor and his wife were expecting me at the exit. After a big hug, we went to a cozy restaurant to celebrate our reunion, having not seen each other since forever.

I met Chongor many years ago at an Egyptian exhibition. We got talking, but so intensely that we didn't even notice the whole day passing as we did so. We went through the museum together and discussed all the mysterious subjects of the entire history of mankind, almost from the Big Bang to the present day. This scientific "And have you heard of this or that story" discourse has defined our friendship from the very first moment, setting the tone each time we have called each other since. We always tackle a topic that science can't solve, or can't find an explanation for, or we just don't agree on. That's where we come in! It is our conviction in every version discussed that it is as we explain it!

Our current encounter was no different. Chongor is Transylvanian through and through. He is a tall, strongly built man with a special Szekler sense of humor; his disregard for the pocket knife carrying tradition of his homeland being the one thing off. After all, every Hungarian knows that the Szekler people are identified by always carrying a pocket knife. His brown hair and round face were lit up by his brown eyes, like those of a loyal dog. He sat comfortably in the restaurant's armchair, delving into his latest conspiracy theory, eager to regale me with it. Mayan culture, what with all its mystical tales, has always been our favorite topic. That's what we ended up discussing that day too. I was delighted to delve into our conspiracy theories on "how to explain everything on Earth" again.

My stay there was jam-packed but fruitful. I got what I went there for. The publisher is happy, I'm happy, what more could I ask for? Ah yes, the balance of royalties from my previous book. Being so new to this, I felt puzzled in his glass-covered office in the apparently infinitely tall skyscraper when I held the piece of paper in my hand. My face contorted in astonishment and I stared at the balance sheet in mute shock.

"Never! It's not a mistake. What you see is exactly correct. The girls in accounting are always spot on!" John said, sitting up straight by way of projecting the professionalism of his firm. John was my contact at the company, a bit reserved but friendly nonetheless.

"Congratulations, Mrs. Breitkreutz. Your book has been a raging success. I think we could go to the next level to enjoy our continued success. The company also offers you a contract for your next book. The secretary has already prepared it" He pushed the stack of papers over to me as he continued to speak. I lost my bearings in the sudden change. An image crossed my mind, of me hunting for publishers with my books not too long ago, and now, they are hunting me down. Have I done something right or was it just blind luck? How could I become so successful in such a short time? The next moment, John's voice yanked me back into the present moment.

"We thought – since we had read your interests – that lucid dreaming could be an interesting topic for your next book. What do you think, would it work? "John asked, saucer-eyed.

"Uh. I haven't dealt with this topic for a long time, and I presume that my knowledge is outdated, as science has advanced since then, and I haven't been practicing this skill for a long time. But I can dust it off if you feel this might be an interesting topic."

"You wrote in your synopsis that you had attained some results with this experiment. Is this true?"

"Of course. But every person works differently. It was very time consuming for me. And the negative thoughts of a stressful lifestyle only left me with depressing dreams. Nevertheless, I felt that I had genuinely solved many problems in my dreams, which had a positive effect on every day of my life."

"Well, I hope the time available will be enough. According to the contract, we cannot deviate from it. On the other hand, your experience of lucid dreaming can provide a great foundation, I feel," John said, nodding. "I'm sure we'll have an exciting book to look forward to."

"Can you give me another clue as to what story to link the lucid dreaming to?" I acquired it tentatively.

"I'll leave that to you, Lina. Find the one that suits you." John ended the exchange cheerfully, and, standing up from the desk, we shook hands. Then he escorted me out of the office, listing all the necessary instructions.

As I stepped out of the office building, I called my husband immediately.

"Hello dear! Well, guess what's just happened to your wife?" I asked Paul excitedly.

"Ahh... Give me a break, will you! Have you been at the publisher? Are you done? What did he say? Tell me!"

"He offered me a contract for my next book!"

"Is this for real?"

"Yup! And you won't believe what the numbers on my royalty checks are. But you can choose! Do you want to eat caviar for breakfast every day for the rest of your life, or do we buy clean water for the people of an African country for a month? What do you want?" I asked with a wild stare because I myself hadn't come to terms with the weight of the situation. Paul laughed at the options, then continued:

"I'll pass on the caviar, but come home and find out what to do."

"All right, sweetie. I'll be there soon, but today I'm still celebrating with Chongor and all."

"Okay, call me when your plane leaves. I love you."

"I love you too."

*

I packed in slo-mo, under the haze of a slight hangover, then headed home. The Mayan time travel with extraterrestrials is a completely barmy theory that me and Chongor made up. Maybe I shouldn't have ordered my third champagne... after all the shots I had! On this occasion, my makeup spruced up my paltry showing juuust enough for that fresh-out-of-rehab look.

On the way home at the airport, a security lady leaned over and asked me softly:

"Do you happen to be the European writer who wrote the book *The Queen and Slave*"?

"Yes, I am," I said, beaming. "Oh, fame is beginning to catch up with me..."

"May I have an autograph please?"

"Of course!" I said and saw she had already taken out her sheet of paper. "What is your name?"

"Theresa," she replied, excitedly. "You know, ma'am, you have helped me a lot. Because of the thoughts you write about in your book, I have gone through a lot of positive changes," she looked at me gratefully.

"Oh, really? I'm very happy about it. You know, I think that was my goal with that book!" I ended the conversation and gave her a note, on which I wrote my best wishes: "To my dearest Theresa from the airport: Lina R. Breitkreutz."

I was grateful to have had the opportunity to meet a person whose life had taken a positive turn because of my book.

HOW TO MAKE YOUR HUSBAND ANGRY

"I'd like to go home to see Mom. We would go out to the country house together, she could do with a bit of fresh air after all this time in the city. And maybe I would be inspired to start a new book. I haven't even written a single line, and my submission deadline is looming nearer every day. This is starting to make me feel tense," I told Paul at dinner, wondering if I should mention my plan to find the castle's owner, just for the sake of curiosity.

"Good idea. But I can't go with you right now. We need to finish the project; the customer is a real asshole. How long do you want to go home for?"

"One or two weeks, tops. It's okay if you can't come now. You know, when I get a book idea, I just pace up and down in a daze until I come up with of a meaningful story," I told him, cringing.

"Yes, I know," Paul laughed. "You are in another dimension anyway. Go ahead. It will be good for your mom too if you spend some time with her. But no getting sidetracked at the cake shop!"

I laughed at Paul's strict exhortation and thanked my lucky stars for having such an understanding and easygoing husband. In the evening, having searched the castle's topographical number – thanks to online administration – I downloaded the property deeds from a database. All official information on the identity of the owners is displayed there. So I packed up and got into the car the next day to get home.

*

After a busy and tiring week behind us, I was sitting on the porch with my mom. The small wooden cabin had shaped up quite well by the beginning of summer. Dad did a good job back when he figured out what the garden should look like. I'll never forget when he bought the plot and we came together to see it. He bought a huge, rectangular jungle. The vegetation was so prolific that it was hard to cut a path among the trees. He spent three summers working on it to made it look presentable. Then came the small chalet project. But the fence couldn't be finished, because lung cancer is cruel, and makes no exceptions. That left me with the care of the garden and the little house. Satisfied, mom and I found it had been a good idea to plunder the local gardening supplier for spring flowers. The rock garden facing us was marvelous with its beautiful, brightly colored flowers. We rested. At least I did, mentally. It was good to put work aside for a little while. But now it'll be time to get back to reality. I'll need a topic that I can link to the publisher's expectations. Although the present state of the castle is much more interesting to me right now. I threw the laptop open on the garden table and, after a little research, found the contact's phone number. After a concise exchange, we arranged the meeting for Tuesday. At the end of our weekend getaway, my mom and I had a barbecue in the evening where we grilled some yummy marinated meat. We drank red wine to go with dinner while waxing nostalgic about my childhood memories. Although we lived in separate worlds – as times change – we had both had the same childhood problems: school stories, boys, friends, family.

"Remember mom, when I wanted Cleopatra hairdo in sixth grade?" Looking back now, I looked terrible.

"Not true. That hair was a very good match for your brown eyes. Rather, it was awkward when I was called to go into the school because of your hair. The headmistress questioned me how I could have dyed your hair when you were just 12. And I didn't even know how to explain that it was because of the summer sun that you had blondish-gingery streaks of hair." I laughed at Mom's story. Poor thing, what she had to endure because of me.

"And do you remember that when you were in second grade and everyone at the fancy dress party was a fairy, a flower and a princess, but you told me to sew a skeleton costume for you?"

"Oh?" Really, how awkward.

The area echoed all night with our laughter. But that wasn't a problem, as we were the only ones at the top of the small village hill. The surrounding fields and the vineyards were our neighbors.

*

The organ bushes arched over the sidewalks in the May breeze. A winding road led up the mountain. At the address given, there was an already-closed bed and breakfast with a single car in its parking lot.

"Greetings! It was me you talked to me a few days ago," I started breaking the ice with a tall, brown-haired, aging woman.

"Good Afternoon! Yes. Come on, let's go to the office."

We went inside, and, already initiating conversation in the corridor, she began asking me questions.

"What do you want to know about the castle? You're not a journalist, are you, and neither are you from National Heritage? Because if so, then we can end the conversation here," she said categorically.

"No. I'm a little more complicated than that, I think. You know, I was there with my husband in January. It's in quite a state, that's a fact. I wanted to ask about this because this building could be so wonderful. And the horror stories I read on the Internet, I'd be curious about those too."

"Sorry, but you haven't come with the intention to purchase?" She asked me a question I suddenly didn't know how to answer. But I didn't want to be turned away, so I went along with the stupid situation just to get the info I wanted.

"Yes, even that is possible. But that would have been a little hasty without knowing the details of such a huge real estate."

"You're right," she conceded as she sat down in the office. "Please sit down. So, the castle currently has two owners, both of German nationality. I am only the contact person for the company, so I cannot decide on any official matters, I can relay official notifications at most. The owners are investors, which is why they bought this building. However, the company profile has changed in the meantime, so they don't have time to work on this project.

Plans for the castle were completed for almost 20 years, but they have since become obsolete. They wanted to sell the building a couple of years ago, but no one came forward because of the high price. I told them that too, and they agreed to rethink my insight. If you are interested in the property now, you might be able to get a better quote. I will be happy to help you because I too regret to see this castle being destroyed. I was down there late last summer because of the local government. It would take a lot of work and money to renovate it, and I'm sure it would be very fortunate if anyone decided to take care of it…"

She kept on talking and talking about the castle. I practically soaked up her words so I could find out every little detail. Meanwhile, the imagined specter of the building came to my mind, until, at a careless moment, my desires won out over my common sense.

"I want to buy the castle!" I blurted out with a sudden determination, interrupting her. "Sorry to butt in, but I have decided I need this house!"

"Castle, if I may ask…" she corrected me stiffly.

"Yes, castle," I hurried our conversation. "Can we talk about the price, please?"

"Of course. I'll look up the records of our last correspondence with the owners. Here it is. At the last real estate valuation, it was worth only HUF 65 million."

"How much is that in euros? Please wait!" I did a quick mental calculation. "Around € 215,000."

"Yeah, that's about it!"

"All right. My offer to purchase is on, but not for that amount. Because I would like to have the property valued too. I think it likely that its value deteriorated some even beyond last year's condition. You understand, don't you?"

"Of course. When you receive the value, contact me and I will relay your offer immediately. Also, if I have to, I'll get all the paperwork ready for the property."

"Thank you in advance. Could I ask – if this would have any positive effect – would you mention to the owners that my husband is also German? Perhaps that would have a positive effect on their decision."

"I'll do my best, ma'am," she said, with a small nod.

Having completed the pro forma dialogue, I drove home to our apartment in Pest. By the time I got there, I'd realized what I'd done: placed a bid for a house large enough to accommodate ten families. Even more so! What will I renovate it from when I only have money to buy it? Such a big house is a hefty responsibility. There are many maintenance costs. Taxes, and so on? "Lina, this is crazy!" Said my common sense. "Oh my God! My husband will kill me when he finds out. That's for sure, I'm finished! But they might still reject my bid," I began to reassure myself. "Or I won't send it at all. What have you done, Lina, are you out of your mind?" My hand began to tremble on the steering wheel. It's one thing that I'm crazy and want to go through with this, but how am I going to present it to Paul?

*

The first company I found online I entrusted with the value of the real estate. I received it, along with a hefty bill for the extra speedy procedure I'd asked for. Its present value is HUF 60 million. At this price, I made my bid, with the new valuation attached. All I had to do was wait for her answer. "Great," I thought to myself, "Now I'll just have to fight Paul to get my castle."

So, I plucked up all my courage and called my husband.

"Hi dear! How's your mom doing?"

"Hi! Oh, my mom? Great, just great! We chilled a bit and the garden's looking beautiful now by the weekend house."

"And when are you coming home? You know, I'm missing my wife!"

"Well… uh, there's a slight problem. I mean…" My voice trailed off.

"What's the matter?"

"No worries! I would just stay home for another week or two.

"But why?"

"You know, I went to see the woman who is the manager of the castle. She's the secretary or something. And so it happened that…"

"What?" Paul's voice was already tinged with suspicion. I knew I wasn't going to get away with what was coming next.

"I made a random bid for the house!" At that moment I fell silent and awaited my fate. After a moment's silence, I'd braced myself for the imminent storm.

"You've done WHAT?" His voice became shrill with indignation, then he continued as I'd expected.

"Clapperboard 112 – war scene," I thought to myself.

"You made an offer? For purchase?" He began shouting.

"I did."

"How could you do that? We haven't even discussed it!" He was beside himself. "And what about my morning caviar? Or the thirsty children in Africa?" He continued, with sarcasm in his voice. "You didn't even think about that either. You didn't even talk to me about it. This is idiotic. Didn't you realize I was your husband? You didn't even want to talk to me about it? There is nothing to renovate or maintain it with."

I held the phone slightly away from my ear, but I could still hear him clearly. I couldn't interrupt or object because I knew he was right. Paul is a chill person, there's never a loud word spoken between us, but then again I've never done anything this barmy before, so I guessed he was not going to take it well.

"I just… please don't be mad at me… I know I should have told you." That is, talk to you in advance.

"How on Earth would I not be mad! I find what you did hurtful. We're a couple. We must make such serious decisions together. And now there you are telling me that you have just *made an offer*," his tone mimicked mine, mockingly.

"I know this looks stupid to you, and to everyone else. But that house is beautiful. I really want to buy it. I don't know why, don't even ask, but I quite simply need it."

"Bah!" he quipped. "When I'm done with the project here, I'll go over there and get you home before you do anything even more stupid."

"But I want this house!" I snapped hysterically, and for a moment both of us fell silent in shock. Then Paul started laughing on the phone.

"Seriously? You are like a hysterical girl throwing a tantrum for her doll."

"Yes, because you are not listening to me! Come on over when you're done with the project. Let's go there again and take a look at it. Please. I want to make you see it's going to be good. We'll figure out the rest together. Or, if you don't want to, it's going to be boring to go it alone because I don't know which room you'll want for your study." I stressed my resolve to show him how serious I was.

"You haven't even bought it, you little dreamer. Don't run so far ahead! They may not even sell it to you."

"When will you come?" I asked, changing the subject for the sake of the peace.

"When I know the project is done, I'll call you straight away. But now I'm angry with you, you know?"

"Yes, I know. But I love you even if you hate me right now."

"I don't hate you, I just don't like it when you're being barmy."

"Then call me, whenever" I hung up with a sigh. I've survived it. I've won the first war! In time, however, he will reconcile with my new passion. But somehow I will have to make amends. It was really reckless of me not to run the idea past him. I should have told him sooner. But there was never a suitable moment. Well, okay, I knew there would be trouble anyway.

*

Two weeks later, an email came from the lady.

"Dear Lina! A response has arrived from the owners, please read the original text below. Congratulations! Looks like you are about to enter a successful real estate purchase. Please call us for the contract details as soon as possible.

Yours,"

Success. I sat stunned in my living room armchair. What shall I do now? Running around mountains of admin, renovations, archaeologists, heaps of money. I don't even know how to do this. What's the first step, or the second? Did I need this?

Mom popped into the room and asked anxiously:

"Are you tired? You look so drawn."

"No, Mom ..." I said wearily, "you know ... it looks like I've bought a castle!"

CHAPTER 5

WITHOUT PHYSICS

I spent days trawling the internet to brush up on the current research results on lucid dreaming. Meanwhile, my memories from various stages of my life bobbed to the surface of my consciousness. In the 2000s, I had not found anything on the Internet about this subject, only one book, entitled "Creative Dream" by Professor Paul Tholey, found its way to me. The contents of the book have grown sketchy in my mind since, so I have read it again. But now, thanks to the internet, videos have been a great way to organize knowledge on lucid dreaming. I found information on the basics, on how-to practical techniques, and everything else all the way to the professional level. Although, to this day, I cannot decide whether what I did in my childhood was in fact lucid dreaming, or some other thing that went beyond it. I wondered.

It happened that when I was a child, I had learning difficulties as early as second grade. When I was a little girl my mother sat down to study with me, but I quickly got confused and lost interest. It was 1986-87. The great communist parenting habits in school, like when I got a huge slap in the face from a teacher for no reason but that he was just explaining to a colleague "how much better my results would be if I wasn't so lazy," sapped me of all motivation.

That's why it happened that I was forced to try to learn what I should have at school in the afternoons slouching at the desk in my room. It was so boring that I found it much more exciting to "get out of my body". At times like those, I moved away from myself and flew to the corner of my room. From here I could see myself sitting at the table trying to study. Those times, when no one was at home, I flew around all corners of the apartment. I did this countless times, and when Mom was home and heard her coming in to my room, I quickly flew back to my body because I thought I'd scare her. After the umpteenth time, I gathered my courage and told her, "Mom, I can fly."

"Yes, honey? I'm very happy about that," she said. But since she received it so naturally, I thought it was not a bad thing to do. Ergo, I could go on doing it. I even tried to explain it to my brother in my little seven-year-old way. "You just bow your head, close your eyes and get out of your body. Do you understand? "In retrospect, it seems funny enough I chill I was about it. My brother, then eight, explained to me, "Ah, this is stupid, such things do not exist. People can't fly! You're a baby, go play with your dolls instead!"

Then my dreams came.

My first strange dream was that my brother and I were in the living room at Christmas and started jumping with joy. But that leaping around was as strange as watching a video of astronauts walking on the moon. In my dream too, at first there was hardly any gravity. In fact, it then stopped altogether because I fell back down so slowly. I almost had to will it to happen. I wanted to get back down on the carpet so I could stand there. Still, it is normal for us to stand and not float, I thought in my dream. Here was my first realization that I was not in reality, but in my own dream. Then I kept on jumping because the experience seemed funny. From then on, lucid dreaming became a regular part of my life. I was afraid of the window when I was awake. We were living on the fifth floor, and all of the windows overlooked the huge, U-shaped courtyard curbed by the main boulevard at the front. The U-shaped courtyard served to connect two houses that my great-grandfather had designed in the 1900s. At that time, by way of payment for engineering this, he received an over 250 square meter apartment. Later it was split in two and we lived in the smaller, 70 square meter part. But in my childhood, those 70 square meters seemed enormous. My mother always warned us never to go near the window, and especially not to climb from the couch up to the window. This made me fearful, so I was even afraid to go near the window in my dreams.

But one time, when I was dreaming, and I knew I was, after the umpteenth try, I took courage and climbed out the window. At first, I clung to the ledge because I was scared to fall. But I didn't feel my weight pulling me into the abyss, because it too had ceased to exist. I began to fancy myself as spiderwoman. We are still in '87 here, so there was no trace of the film world yet – since our first TV arrived in our home in '88 – or comic books, as they hadn't arrived in the land at that time. Then I decided I was able to kneel on the wall of the house as if it were a parquet floor, then started to climb on it on all fours. I was so circumspect that I even remembered not to let the neighbors on the opposite side see me, or else they'd get a heart attack from witnessing a kid crawling around the wall on the fifth floor...

I crawled around like this a few times in my dreams on the wall of a building, defying the laws of physics.

Then remember us one day going over to the neighbors who lived on the third floor on the opposite side of the building. Our parents had a pleasant chat and my brother and I challenged the two girls to a pillow fight. It was incredibly fun to make such a mess as a kid as a kid and play in such a carefree way. This gave me such a high that in my dream I started wondering if the girls were having a pillow fight over there again. So, the next time I was crawling on the wall in my dream, I suddenly kicked myself away from the wall to fly over to the one of the house opposite. I acted in full confidence, knowing that I would be slowing down on the way before I get across. So, with a single bound, I effortlessly leapt thirty meters from the fifth floor to the third on the other side. It's wrong to peep, but my curiosity got the better of me. It was depressing to see them sitting cramming at the table. Maybe I should be doing this too instead of flying back and forth? But this is such a good feeling. I feel so unbounded and infinite at those times. As if I could do anything I wanted.

I told mom about my experiences again, because she didn't mind last time. "Mom, imagine now I can fly in the courtyard and jump over to another wall, to the house opposite." She calmly acknowledged this too until one day she sat me down for a serious conversation a few months later.

"Honey, can you just tell Mom what that flying lark is all about? You know we talk about everything, so rest assured I won't be angry."

"Well, it was like I learned in my dream."

"Yeah, but what exactly do you do then?"

"I don't know, Mom, it just works easily. Now in my dream I just go to the window of the living room, climb up and jump out. But I never fall, but I fly wherever I want to," I said with a proud smile.

Mom turned white as a sheet and, with an anguished, tortured expression, began to admonish me.

"Sweetheart, I'd like to ask you to never fly again in your dream!"

"But why, Mom?" My heart began to sink at the thought of being deprived of such happiness, and I did not understand why she did so either.

"You know, my treasure, when people sleep, their bodies are in bed, resting. We dream of all kinds of beautiful things. But your body has not yet learned how to relax, so you sometimes get up in your dreams. This is called sleepwalking! You don't remember it, but Dad and I always see you walking around in the evenings. Then we always take you back to your bed and you keep on sleeping. But it can be dangerous if we fall asleep and do not realize that you are walking around. You know, I love you very much and I would be very sad if anything happened to you. That is why I would like to ask you to never fly in your dream again, and never go to the window even in your dream!"

That's when my childhood "flying adventures" ended, to my chagrin. And this is where the scare of the figure emerging from the shadow of the piano went away too. Every night when I woke up, my body couldn't move for a few moments. This is called sleep paralysis, which I didn't understand at the time, but it was as if I'd been born with this knowledge. I knew if I waited patiently for a few seconds, my body would be able to move, and the wickedly moving shadow would disappear too. Of course, until those few moments passed, the fear of defenselessness overwhelmed me so much that I will never forget it.

*

Many, many years later, in my twenties, I read Professor Tholey's book and tried to interpret it. It was then that I started practicing lucid dreaming again. This is where I learned to categorize my various dreams. I have plain dreams, which were meant to reveal to me the entangled ephemera of daily events. They made no sense at all. These were always dreams in black and white. Taking my mother's generation as my starting point and studying the dream book of Gyula Krúdy, I first put my dreams into two categories. Black and white dreams are meaningless ones that I can immediately discard. But the colorful ones always carried some information. But not always, not even those. I received symbols connected to the events of my daily life, whose meaning I meditated on, trying to draw parallels with my life. These symbols made my life a lot easier. Then the next category was of dreams of the future. At first I didn't know what it was about my dream that was strange after I woke up, but a thought struck me: note what it feels like and wait for it to come true. A few weeks or months later, when I indeed found myself in the situation, I remembered that this had already happened. After a few such occurrences, I started to pay very close attention, and soon I was able to categorize each of my dreams after waking up. I used my lucid dreams to connect with my loved ones who had passed away. Before this learning phase began the time in my life when my family had to go to a funeral almost every year because we'd lost someone. To this day, I keep in touch with my loved ones who have gone over to the other side. Every time I dream about them, they always provide me with useful information to use in my life. Well, it's time for me to keep a dream diary again, and I feel I have to come up with reality check techniques too.

CHAPTER 6

THE SIXTH ORPHAN

After a couple of days of research, I asked for an appointment with the local town historian where the castle was located. Then, by way of a cardio training session, I walked up to the archives at the gate of the beautiful Buda Castle. In the reading room, I could only hear the rustling sound of pages being turned by people sitting at tables. Not a breath or the slightest movement. I was careful not to break the order of silence by accident, so I tiptoed over to the lady behind the desk and whispered to her. Since I had previously requested the material on the Internet, I was just waiting to thumb through the huge bundles that could be evidence of past events. No matter what, I wanted to find some information about that strange, mysterious family who built that castle. I found the weighty correspondence of the Nedeczky family, as well as a lock of Francis Deák's hair and his correspondence with Ida Nedeczky. He seemed to be embarrassingly affectionate towards his great niece. Although this is not surprising for this age when men married their nieces to protect family property. It is interesting how the tone of his letter changed after Ida wrote of her future engagement with Alexander Szabadhegyi. There was another letter from the old man, to Emma Nedeczky, Ida's older sister. It informs Emma of his arrival at her husband's funeral.

I tried to put together a picture of what the family tree might look like. At that moment, my phone started flashing. It was John's call, so I ran out of the hallway to pick it up in time.

"Hi, John! How can I help?"

"Hello, Lina! How have you been lately?"

"Good, thank you. I'm working on a new story. How about you?"

"Very well! Do you know why I called, Lina? I would like to be the first to congratulate you before you receive your honorarium by email. It's fantastic to see another book of yours amongst the top sellers in four months," he shouted cheerily.

"You're kidding, aren't you? This book too? Oh my God! It's unbelievable!"

I almost started jumping for joy like a kid, it made me so happy.

"I wonder if your new book will do even better than anything else you've written so far," John said, laughing on the phone.

"So do I, John!" Thank you for calling.

"Keep up the good work, Lina."

We hung up and I paused for a moment: "Do better than anything so far?"

That will be something else indeed. I went back to the reading room with mixed feelings tinged with worry, and thought I would wait for Paul to tell him the good news in person.

CAVIAR OR WATER?

Paul's plane landed at half past three, and I waited for him impatiently in the parking lot. On the way home, I could hardly wait to finally have a chance to tell him all about my phone call with John because he was regaling me with the details of unveiling his projects. Then he began to nag me to make me change my mind about buying the castle, since we still have no money to do it up it anyway. Then came the moment:

"Are you sure?" I smiled mysteriously. Intrigued, Paul smiled back.

"You know, Sweetheart, I talked to the publisher yesterday…" I paused for a dramatic break here.

"*The missed Waltz* has become a success too!" I grinned like the Cheshire cat, and, with not a hint of false modesty, continued: "Sorry, honey, I can't really help being this good. You know, it's my fault, maybe I shouldn't be writing such a-mazing books!"

"Of course, of course!" Paul said with a smile.

"Would you allow me to inaugurate your statue and pray to you, Your Holiness then? Or should I just call you Majesty"?

"A daily kiss on my hand will suffice!" We laughed at my overacting, then he asked with a grin,

"How much did you get?"

"Enough to have your study picked and furnished first if we bought the castle."

"But we'd have to do it all up first!"

"Yes, and we can start the renovations easy-peasy, and don't forget that I'm in the throes of my next book now."

"Be real, that's nowhere near finished yet!"

"Good, but it will be, and make it to the top of the list too! Do you want to come with me to get the paperwork done?"

"Not really. I still think it's unnecessary to throw away that much money on this, but if you want, let's go. But let's just stop somewhere to eat or else I'll eat you!" Paul began to tickle me.

"No, I'll cause a crash!"

"Okay, good."

After a soul-soothing silence he quipped:

"Well, okay!" If you are this crazy, then I insist that the renovation of the house go according to my plans! He acquiesced, having finally given up the fight against my dream.

I looked at my husband silently and gratefully, who returned a gaze filled with selfless love to me. A wave of gratitude washed over me for being so lucky as to be able to live my life with him.

THE LADY IN THE BLUE DRESS

We left the lawyer's office with a smallish folder, which contained all the castle-related papers, from the sales document and the deeds to the papers handed over by the former owners.

We headed straight to the small town on the motorway straight away to visit our newly acquired ruins as its official owners. It's more than two hours' drive from the capital to our new home, but I didn't mind. On the way, I tried to contain my excitement. A huge house with a huge responsibility and lots of money to be spent transforming it into a truly habitable home. I think, knowing myself, it's too much of a luxury to have such a big house. In addition, we do not even live in Hungary. But I'll definitely spend a lot of time here, that's for sure.

We turned again onto the dirt road well-worn by tractors. The turret of the house now seemed even more dilapidated and foreboding because of the weight of the responsibility that its renovation carried. But that feeling was outweighed by the happiness I felt. I enjoyed the idea that I didn't even know where to start the actual designing work of which room should be assigned to what. Where should our beautiful library be? Where will our bedroom be? Where will Paul's office be? What condition is the cellar in? I'd browse through the technical drawings to see where the water pipes ran or where the electrical wiring was in the walls. How long will it take for the external repair work to be completed? How massive a heart attack will the construction engineer get on seeing the state of the walls?

We stopped in front of the door. I grabbed Paul's hand and we stepped over the hole in the ground where the gate should have stood.

"We're home, baby!" I said, squeezing his hand.

"We'll be reliving this moment when the house is ready!" He smiled and then we headed up the stairs. The cold, grubby walls patchily defaced by vandals screamed of neglect. A crumbling partition here and there, with heaps of bricks at the bottom. The window frames were completely missing in some places, and the creepers growing in the upstairs balcony window and colonizing the interior of the house made the view from the inside even more bizarre.

While taking pictures, we suddenly spotted a female figure in the other half of the living room. Startled, all three of us stopped, and spoke to each other in muted voices.

"Good afternoon!" I felt it apt to start the conversation being the owner, even though of course the strange lady didn't know of this. I sized up the lady in the blue summer dress from afar, with her light brown hair tied back in a tasteful bun.

"To you too!" She greeted me in a friendly voice.

"I see, we're not the only ones who are impressed by this house!" I carried on.

"Indeed not. I've been looking at pictures of it on the internet for a long time. This ruin is simply wonderful and gruesome in one. You know, I mean the owners who have neglected it like this."

"Yes, I agree," I said. And as we got closer to each other, I saw that I was chatting with a very nice, friendly lady.

"Do you like it too?" she asked.

"Shall we be on first name terms?" I think it would be easier. Unfortunately, my partner does not speak Hungarian but German. This is Paul, and I'm Lina. We shook hands.

"Oh, all right. I'm Christie, hi." She looked at Paul, nodding.

"Yes, we really like it too. We have been here once before in the winter. You're not a journalist or anything, right?" I asked distrustfully.

"Oh no, not at all. I'm a teacher. We were heading out with the kids, but then at the last minute they changed their minds and went to the beach with their dad. They've always loved going for a dip."

"Yes, I can imagine that. Kids love to paddle. Mine loved it too when she was little." We smiled at each other.

We got chatting from the first moment. Christie exuded such calm and friendliness that I felt like we had known each other for a thousand years. I also saw she felt the same, so it was clear that we would be exploring the castle together. Skipping all the normal rounds of pleasantries, we shared all kinds of personal details with each other in five minutes. Just like times when two friends haven't met in a long time, and they need to make up for lost ground quickly. Having assessed my friend of five minutes as harmless, I decided to trust her.

"How would you renovate this house if it were yours?" I asked, hoping to stir her imagination.

"Well... I'd know what to do with it, for sure." Her face lit up. "I would like to have beautiful wallpaper. Look, there was a place for the stove. I would have it rebuilt, of course. Uh, my kids would love it. Here they would play hide and seek all day in the living room and on the terrace all day. And I'd definitely make one room all red. And the upstairs room in the turret would definitely be my own little nook. Have you been upstairs to see the view? It is wonderful. You can see half of Lake Balaton from there."

"We haven't been up yet."

"And you? What would *you* do with it?" Christie asked.

"Something like what you said. But first, I think we need to do some external repairs. Renovate the roof and only then can we move on to the interior."

"How prepared you are," she smiled. "You say this as if this were your castle."

I looked at her, smiling quietly. Then I reached out my hand and we symbolically shook hands again.

"Welcome to our house! We are the new owners. And you seem to be our very first guest. I'll never forget this!"

As Christie shook hands with me, she froze in shock, but her face told us all we needed to see. Happiness to meet the new owner because, a new owner means that the house might be changing. Someone who came here to get something going with this ruin.

"My God, this is incredible! Then the house has a chance to survive! I'm very, very pleased to hear that. It's so terrible to even see it vandalized to have it destroyed as quickly as possible."

"Yes, I know. We will immediately begin the fencing off and the first steps of the renovations so that they cannot destroy it any more. Getting the paperwork and permissions processed is likely going to take a long time, but I'll try to keep nagging the office to get all the necessary paperwork as soon as possible. I don't like to faff about with official stuff, so I'll be quick."

"Nah, nor do I," said Christie. "I don't like to get bogged down with official things either."

"Ah. Have you read the ghost stories about the castle?" I asked.

"I have… quite scary. In fact, I find the story so exciting that I've started writing a book about it," said Christie. "I've collected a lot of background material about the whole castle and its inhabitants."

"Seriously?"

"Yup. Let's swap phone numbers and email addresses and if you are interested, I will be happy to share what I found with you. I have even been at the local archives."

"I was at the one in Budapest," I replied with a smile.

"Huh, and what have you found?"

"One or two bits of correspondence from family members. A hugely elaborate family tree…things like that. I bought a photo ticket for a day and photographed all the papers. I'll send it to you, you must see it all. So you write, too?"

"Why? You too?"

"The thing is, that is what I do for a living, actually. I'm a writer."

"My God!" exclaimed Christie. "This is the best birthday present I've ever had!"

"Is it your birthday today? Well…" I said in shock. "In that case, I wish you a happy birthday!"

"Thank you, I'm so glad we met today. You know, I don't believe in coincidences. For some reason it was important for us to meet," Christie said with an air of mystery.

I wholeheartedly agreed with her. I also felt that this was not an ordinary encounter and that we definitely had a role to play in each other's lives. I like to make decisions based on my intuition. It always points me in the right direction. The three of us talked for another couple of hours and ended up hanging out at the local pastry shop, to Paul's great delight. Christie was not at all uncomfortable knowing that we were wealthy, which put me at ease. After all, people get embarrassed when they suspect the other person has a lot of money. I know, because way back when I was embarrassed. The afternoon went so well that our new friend invited us to the next meeting.

"If you think you'll have time, we could meet again. How long are you staying? I could introduce you to my family and we could go out with the kids to ride a horse-drawn carriage. My sister and her family keep horses."

My eyes lit up at the prospect of this exciting adventure, and I immediately translated our new friend's request for Paul, who smiled and nodded at the idea.

"That's very kind of you. Yes, we might just take you up on that. Thank you very much in advance."

"Well, I have to get going, the kids are at home with their dad."

"Yes, so do we. We've had quite a busy day. I'm very glad we met you. We could talk more about the ghosts next time, and about the furnishings of the house. I think your taste must be very sophisticated, so I'm sure I'll ask for your help."

"Good idea. I will be happy to help you."

At the entrance of the house where we were parked, we waved to each other cheerfully, and I spent the entire drive to the hotel singing Christie's praises to Paul. I had never encountered such a pleasant creature before. She radiated such tranquility and poise. Her entire being was so collected. She practically oozes intelligence and sophistication. Her round, gentle face with those big blue eyes is really appealing. Many men must be dreaming of this type of woman. As a woman, I rarely praise women's virtues, but Christie clearly deserves it. I am determined to be very good friends with her.

Paul just smiled at my exuberance at meeting a new person. As we prepared for dinner, the expected email also arrived, with lots of attachments and the first few chapters of the book she'd started.

We went to bed at night and I couldn't wait to start reading:

"Time is tearing me apart, I feel like a thing of the past.

My treasures are weeping, weeping in the dust.

The killer breeze marks my wounded flesh

with abandon, and silence grows in me.

My loneliness – my fort forever,

the sixth orphan, I was delivered... "

The wonderful Lake Balaton

I promised Paul a great walk and hike to show him how wonderful the surroundings of Lake Balaton are. The masts of sailboats rocking in the harbors could be seen even from the village. The rows of vineyards and the cultivated lands on the hills alternated wonderfully in an array of different colors. He liked the area, which put a spring in my step, because we also have something to boast of to match the majestic German mountains. We vied to show off landscapes from our respective countries – Hungary, being largely flat, cannot lay claim to mountains as high as those in Germany. But, we do have our wonderful Lake Balaton, which, besides the many summer festivals and events, provides an unforgettable experience for all visitors.

We had to decide with a game of rock-paper-scissors which wine cellar to pick for the wine tasting. According to the Internet, there are eighty-four wine cellars around Lake Balaton and they all offer excellent wines. So it happened that we tasted the range offer thoroughly in the wine cellar of the next village. The owner was arguing with the chef in one corner because he was the wrong side of tipsy. Even so, we were served the world's finest stew that night. I didn't miss the opportunity to rub

Paul's nose in the fact that this was real stew and not what the Germans are trying to imitate under the name of Goulash. As the evening drew in, the youngsters at one of the tables began singing, cuing the whole crowd of guests in the cellar. It was a big surprise that the young generation is singing the Kiss King by Hungária and other songs by them, because this hit swept through the country back in the '70s, and even my generation shook its booty to it at the start of the millennium. Apparently, it has become an evergreen all-time hit. We stumbled home to our accommodation that day in good cheer. I really love wine cellars where the owner is friendly, direct, and always knows how to talk a person into having another glass or three. I don't reckon there can be any tourists, save one or two, who might leave of a wine cellar empty-handed, as everyone always finds something to their taste. The next day, of course, shaped up to be far slower-paced. According to local lore, the best medicine to counter the power of Hungarian wines is real Hungarian broth, which we soothed our stomachs with at the local restaurant. Then we ended up in the Hévíz Thermal Baths and enjoyed doing precisely nothing.

THE BUTLER WITH THE WHITE GLOVES

Having explored the area thoroughly in the summer, I was happy to see that Paul likes it here. One morning we started at the castle to receive archaeologists on account of the two mosaics. Our negotiations ran surprisingly smooth, and they agreed to start preparations for the restoration project the following week.

"Way back when we first came here, we had only stumbled into one property. Remember?"

"I do. And now we are in our own ruin. Good. I just can't find my office, Sweetheart," Paul said with a giggle.

"All right, but we're going to build it! I just have no idea where to start..."

"Come on, I'll show you!" Paul grabbed my arm and began to pull me toward the attic stairs. With the same breath, he started his lecture, as if he were at work:

"First and foremost, the garden needs fixing," he said. "We need to call the gardener to tend the protected trees, and to clear out the rest, weeds, thicket and all."

Meanwhile, we reached the attic, where he pointed towards the garden by the window:

"Gardeners know which trees are worth keeping and which ones are not. You will have your swing bed there later if you get tired of gardening. How would you like the flowerbeds to be?" he asked me abruptly, pulling me close with a tango-like move.

"Well, I don't really know... In a large circle or a semicircle in front of the entrance? I want colorful summer flowers and along the edges of the plot with your favorites. I want to make a summer kitchen with a terrace in the shed behind the house. And the hut next door could house your DIY corner."

"Yesss! And we can watch soccer championships in the summer with the boys!"

"Sure..." I smiled at my little soccer crazy German husband.

"What about the house?"

"The roof needs to be redone and the exterior renovation will be the second round. Of course, it all depends on what the engineer says, and what the listed buildings' office may think about the renovation plans… If possible, I would like to keep the doors and windows," I told Paul.

"There is no entrance gate to the house, honey!"

"Yes, I know," I smiled. "We need a new one. But the frames are in place for the windows and doors. If they are not rotten, can I keep them as nice as they are, with their old cassette panels…"

"All right, honey. When the doors and windows are ready, the electricians, the heating and the water system can come. Professionals, planning, etc.. They make a lot of dirt and dust while working, so it's not worth doing the walls and floors until afterwards. In the meantime, you might want to figure out where you want your underfloor heating, and in which rooms you want floor tiles or a parquet. And first we have to figure out what function to give each room."

"Then we'll figure it out, come on," I pulled Paul toward the living room.

As we walked down the corridor between the dusty, cobwebby walls, an idea emerged:

"Before anyone starts any work here, they need a cleaning crew with two skips. We could do it this week as we're staying in the village anyway," Paul said.

"I'll look for a gardening crew too, they could come to survey the terrain," I replied.

"And by then, the renovation company could come, and even if work doesn't start because of the permits, they still have to fence off the area under renovation. Anyway, the paparazzi will be descending here the moment they get sniff of the castle being renovated."

"Yes, you see, I didn't even think of that," I said to Paul. "I'm hungry, let's go to the village to grab a bite! I really liked the last restaurant."

"The one with real Hungarian, greasy, spicy food?" Paul laughed.

"Yup. I exclaimed. I'm going to go for a heart attack on a plate, just because! Something with tons of grease, and no salad! With bread and a truckload of calories! You know I love Hungarian cuisine, by the way, it's much more delicious than German food."

I stuck out my tongue with a sneer: "Yes, I can't argue with you about that."

Walking down the hallway to the living room, we heard a door slamming. We hurried to the living room, where a gray-haired gentleman in a butler's robe stood, clutching a candlestick in his white gloved hands. We both froze, not knowing how to respond to the phenomenon. Wanted to get closer, but the old man shouted:

"Dinner is served!" Then he strode through the door that led to the kitchen.

Paul and I exchanged a look of shock. "What the heck?" We both headed for the door without thinking, tearing it open in his wake, stoked on adrenaline. We both knew that this was neither a hidden camera prank nor a fool in the village who'd dressed us up in full butler garb to scare us. It was clear that the phenomenon itself was completely paranormal.

We parted behind the door and walked through that wing of the house. Not a soul anywhere. Neither the apprentice or his candlestick. We left the castle; I had goosebumps all over.

"I can feel them, of course, but I've never seen one," I said to Paul, stunned.

"We have new residents!" Paul said, without a hint of irony, as he got in the car. "One more of these, and I'll definitely need a change of underwear! Get them to clear off, honey."

Once at the restaurant, we just sat in silence. We caught each other's gaze several times, but somehow could not utter a word. Eventually, Paul broke the silence:

"So then... You're the witch, this is your table to deal with. What was that this afternoon? It is clear that we have no butler, we would know about it if we did. We went around the house too, and such garments are only available through costume rental now, I guess. So what gives? He looked at me, waiting for an explanation."

"Don't think I wasn't petrified! It is one thing to feel ghosts and all kinds of energies without a physical body, and quite another to see a person who seems completely real, who then vanishes into thin air. I don't quite understand the scene either. If it is a ghost, then it is actually haunting the house. We know from crappy ghost flicks that they want to say something, otherwise they wouldn't be there scaring us to death. Or, they just want to scare us. I don't know, we need to find out somehow. Could the old man have died? Because he was wearing something ancient, he surely must be dead. But it does matter if he died a natural or violent death. And anyway, what could be his motivation to be meandering around with a candlestick here, scaring us to death? Anyway, you don't have to be afraid, ghosts mostly just scare you, they don't kill you" I added skeptically "at least I hope they don't..."

"All right, then we'll go tomorrow and buy all the candles and whatever you want and work some magic to keep me from going through this again!"

I chortled. "It does not work that way! I won't do a ritual because a ghost wanted to serve us dinner by chance. First we need to find out who this ghost was. I'll look on the net in what era this type of dress was in fashion. It will help a lot."

"All right," Paul grabbed my hand and smiled sarcastically. "Don't you think you could whip up a juicy little ghost story out of this?"

"Hehehe... What do I do with a ghost we've only seen once? An exciting book requires mysterious deaths, not really the disembodied spirit of a servant."

"Just teasing you, sweetheart," Paul said, sticking his tongue out at me again.

By the evening the order had returned and we were resting at our nearby hotel.

DREAM DIARY

"This is the sixth month that I have been trying different techniques before bedtime and in my waking hours. So far I've had little success. I have achieved so much that I can recall each of my dreams in rich detail after waking up, and they remain vivid in my memory even in the afternoon. I have also come to being able to bring conscious awareness to my dreams. But every time I realize that I am dreaming, I grow so excited that I cannot attend to the plot and wake up. I can only report one success, it happened after many months' trying last night. I dreamed that my husband and I were on the road and stopped to refuel on the highway. Entering the shop, Tibi, a dear old friend of mine, was sitting on the first bar stool of the café area. The interior and colors of the café were strikingly vivid. He was just sipping coffee and as he put his cup down, he turned to me in the chair and smiled. It was at this moment that I knew I was in a dream, because this friend I hadn't seen for years had died in a car accident. Yet he is here before me now, so there is no doubt that I am in my own dream. I walked over to him with a smile and held him tight.

"Wait, I won't let you go yet! Who knows when I'll be able to do this again," I told him while I held him for an embarrassingly long time. After all, we had been really good friends, and his absence weighed heavy on me. Even so, I had processed his loss, so I didn't understand why he was "included" in my dream now.

"How are you these days?" I asked.

"Very well. This coffee is still not my... uh, cup of tea, as it were," he glanced at his black cup and grimaced just as he had done in life. "What about you? I see you're on the road..."

"We are. We're going home." At that moment, it occurred to me that talking to dead people in our dreams is always helpful, as we can get advice on our lives from them. So I quickly changed the subject in aid of this noble cause.

"Do you want to tell your brother anything? You do know that he and everyone else misses you very much, don't you?"

"Yes, I know. Tell him to get more cars no matter what!"

"Okay," I said, puzzled. But I started thinking about what this message could mean. I was so focused on the meaning that the coffee shop scene dissolved in front of me and I woke up.

This morning I called my friend's brother. I told him my dream on the phone, and received a deep silence in response. I was aware that – not having an heir – his brother inherited the delivery company that my friend had left behind, but I never asked them about business.

"You still there?" I asked tentatively, assuming the line was dead.

"Yes I'm here. It's just astonishing!"

"What do you mean?"

"The message. Two orders came in last week and I was thinking that I didn't have enough cars to accept both, and whether I should get more cars or cancel one of the orders!"

Now I was silent for a moment as I'd received the answer to the message in my dream. But then I got past the phenomenon with the understanding that I was right about conversations with the dead again.

"Then go ahead get some more cars," I chuckled into the phone, "since your brother told you what to do!"

"Indeed. What he says is probably true. This will make my decision clear. Heck, I have a call coming in on the other line. We'll talk, okay?"

"All right, enjoy work. Hugs!"

We hung up abruptly.

I didn't mind, because I too had to get used to the new, inexplicable phenomenon. What would dream researchers or scientists say to this? In any case, after my childhood years, I can mark my first success, even if it has been confused with some paranormal message. For me, these things that science deems paranormal – because it can't find an explanation for them – are as natural to me as cherry blossom in the spring.

In the afternoon I checked the mail from Christie, filled with various documents about the castle. Newspaper articles, photographs of ancient documents from the archives, descriptions of the castle in various databases on the Internet, or wherever the castle and its owners had ever been mentioned in some form. So I picked up the first file, which was a report made by the local TV channel with a historian. It listed the residents' sad stories in considerable detail. The lower black castle was built by Stephen Nedeczky around 1860. A few years later, his brother Eugene relieved him of his financial burdens. Then, on the opposite side of the road, Eugene had a small palace built on the hillside on the occasion of his upcoming marriage to his niece, Emma Nedeczky. The wedding took place on February 26, 1881, but due to the strange early death of the young woman, in 1883 Eugene was widowed. He never married again and left no offspring either. Eight years after the tragedy, he completed the construction of the castle, and the building attained its present state. In 1892, Eugene was elected a Member of Parliament, and the impressive, spacious house went well with the title. In 1908, Eugene's brother Stephen died.

The first violent death occurred in 1912, when the shepherd of the house, Stephen Papp, stabbed the cook 13 times. She was 57-year-old Karolina Getri, who worked in the house; the two had been lovers. Stephen got ten years, despite having a good defense lawyer, Dr. Endre Weisz.

The suicide series begins in 1914 with the first owner of the castle. Eugene, having long suffered from his incurable rheumatism in his old age, decides to liberate himself from his mortal coil. So, he "stylishly" shot himself in the head one day before his 74th birthday. As of this date, for the next 14 years, there is no information on the possible inhabitants of the castle. Then the tragedy continues with the new owners. In 1928, Dr. Vág and his wife move to the castle from Budapest. The new owner, who is also a Eugene, commits suicide due to his wife's infidelity. The well driller acquires the title of Lord of the House by taking his place next to the woman as the new man. But the black widow is unaffected by her husband's tragedy, and she carries on in her lustful ways, much to the chagrin of the well driller. When she gets tired of the well driller, she looks for a new lover, in response to which the well driller also commits suicide. According to local rumors, which are not confirmed by official historical records, it is an alleged Adorján Nagy who in the end turned the black widow out of her fortune and then vanished. Thus, the destitute widow divested herself of the castle around 1930. The last private owner was a businessman, Eugene Marich, who died in 1945. He was said to have been spying for the English, and when the German forces arrived in the village, Eugene put an end to his life.

I leaned back in the armchair and shuddered at my newly fashioned conspiracy theories. At that moment, I could no longer be so happy with the house that I wanted to make my new home. Strange coincidences. Two owners named Eugene, both committed suicide. Interestingly, the violent death of a cook survived to see the gaze of posterity, because in that era it was not really fashionable to record anything about serving staff. It is depressing to think the house would be cursed. Yes, people snort derisively when you talk about things like this, but it still seems that men can't be lucky here. I thought of Paul, and my heart ached. I hope he doesn't get hurt. Not a suicidal sort, and I'll never be a black widow. So there is a chance for a peaceful survival ... I hope.

Chapter 8

High heels in New York

I began the evening worn out and beset with stage fright. Just as my plane landed, I hurried to drop off my stuff at the hotel, then got into the waiting car to be taken to the studio. I can't complain, my publisher is doing its best to make me a celebrity. On the way in the car, the assistant told me in detail all the things I couldn't do or say during the show, drawing my attention to the possible legal consequences. By the time I came to my senses, the makeup artist was already busying herself with a sponge all over my face.

"Do I have to get used to this too?" I asked the girl in a flat monotone, but I could see behind her confused smile she didn't understand why I was asking this.

"I don't know," she replied with a modest smile.

I was constantly trying to keep an eye on the assistant, but he was running up and down with his headphones in his ears and he had a terrible, breakneck American accent, so I never knew when he was going to be talking to me or into the phone.

But he cut my wondering short:

"In you go, you're next up. Smile, and listen to the interpreter," he said, then adjusted the thingy in my ear.

"Aaaand nooow give a very warm welcome to Lina R. Breitkreutz, who has been topping our bestseller list for six months!"

I set off for the stage. The crowd in the studio applauded loudly and burst into cheers. My heart nearly jumped out of its place in excitement. Maybe that's a bit too much applause, I thought to myself. My eyes quickly got used to the bright light of the reflectors. They had to, or else I would end up face down on the floor live on air, although I may not be the first one.

"Welcome, Lina. How are you?"

"Good evening everyone, I'm fine thank you. The makeup artist stuffed powder even in my ears, but apart from that all is well."

Jim and the audience smiled and I was trying to hide my nervousness with banter like this.

"First of all, let me ask where this pen name has come from."

"Great question. The name Lina was given to me by a girl friend of mine, and I added the letter R because of the resulting mystical resonance of my name. I believe that a name can have the power to influence a person's life more positively."

"And the name Breitkreutz?"

"My husband's mother's maiden name, which my husband carried on." I thought I could express my respect for my husband's family with this gesture.

"That's really nice," Jim said.

"How do you see your success, Lina?" How do you like your place at the top of the hit lists?

"Well, yes, I like it. At first I didn't believe it. To be more specific, that was the plan, and I've always hoped for it, but now that it's actually here, it's making me really happy."

"You did not believe it?" Jim asked.

"No. When I got my first serious settlement from my agent, I thought something had gone awry in their calculations."

The audience laughed again.

"Tell me, Lina, where did the idea for *The Queen and Slave* and the *Missed Waltz* story come from?"

"I think those who have been following the press know that both stories contain biographical motifs. Nonetheless, the personality development of the character in my first book is truly remarkable. And the *Missed Waltz* is a dainty love story. I formed one of its characters from a real childhood love of mine. Glad the fans like it."

"Which character of *The Queen and Slave* is yours?"

"Both! I think every woman has both good and bad qualities. They can be weak and vulnerable as much as strong and determined. It depends on our personality type and the circumstances of our lives."

"How do you start a story? How does the creation process unfold in your work?"

"Oh," I laughed, before giving my well-rehearsed answer. "Well, that's kind of funny. Most of my books are made up of actual events in my life. I pick out an event or person and mold their personality to fit a given story. Before writing each of my books, I do my planning as a first step. I think it looks funny. In my husband's eyes, this seems like I'm not doing anything for weeks, months, since I don't write a single line. Even so, from morning to night my mind is working on what kind of plot it should be, to whom it should be connected and in what mood. And when the many, many tiny scenes dance in my head, I flood the living room with little notes and scribblings overnight. This is when I make a sketch of the story. By the time I finish this, the scenes develop in my head as to how to describe them. How long they should be, and in what mood. After that, I start writing a chapter completely at random, the one in which I am emotionally involved, the one which I am experiencing and can identify with. It is difficult for me to go through the plot of the book in a linear way, because the mood of the plot is what guides my work. When I'm almost done with the whole raw book, I set it aside for one or two weeks, and when all the tangled thoughts in my head have cleared or settled, I make corrections and when I feel I can release the story because it's ready, I send it to the publisher."

"Very interesting. Now I imagined you scattering sticky notes all over the place."

"Yes," I smiled, "sometimes I toss pens around too if I get stuck," I added, cheerfully.

"Tell me, Lina, is it true that you bought a small castle in Hungary?"

"Yes, that's so."

"Why a castle? I mean, people, when they are wealthy, prefer to buy or build a beautiful, modern house. Then why castles?"

I broke out in a smile by the time the translator translated the question.

"I like old-fashioned buildings and furniture. The style that has been left over from bygone eras. I'm not just thinking about luxury villas. I also like rustic objects. I have a whole collection from a local gardener who also makes wonderful pottery using traditional motifs. Wonderful handcrafted products. But, to get back to the house, I find architectural works outstanding works of art. Unfortunately, there are a lot of neglected castles in Hungary, and I thought that saving even one for posterity counts towards doing something to sustain our culture. Anyway, that's one way I can have a butler. Okay, he is a ghost haunting the place, but at least he exists!" I said with a smile, and the audience burst out laughing.

"Answer me one last question. What story are you working on now?"

"Ah. I don' think a writer can ever answer that question prematurely, but if you want a spoiler no matter what ... you know what? ... Nnnope, I won't say a word!" I laughed.

"That is not fair." I thought we could find out something from you.

"Of course, my publisher would kill me."

"All right, Lina. Thank you for being with us tonight."

"Thank you for being here with you!"

The audience gave a rapturous applause as I shook hands with Jim and then, with pained focus on my gait in the high heels, I left the studio with a smirk on my face.

As I got behind the curtain, I immediately removed my shoes, to which I saw a mix of surprise and amusement on the assistant's face. I paid no heed to it, I just wanted to find the locker room so I could get back to the hotel as soon as possible.

"I've survived it," I thought to myself. I thought I'd die of excitement. Never had so many people look at me at once. Especially, how many millions of people will still see this on TV? I must look terrible on camera.

THE BOX

A few days later, the first-round cleaning brigade arrived. The containers were changed daily on the service road, and the gardeners tidied up the garden nicely. The brigade leader looked at me wide-eyed when I told him on the first day that I had gardening clothes and gloves. I reassured him that I wouldn't be taking part to keep a check on things, but for my own sake, because I really like gardening. Feel free to command me as well as your subordinates, I told him. He scratched his head and replied:

"As you wish, ma'am! Come on guys, let's get to work," he exclaimed, motioning with his huge arms.

I got covered in dirt from head to toe by the end of each day. I was sweating, my back hurt, and the scratches on the thorny bushes and branches did not spare me either. But after the shrubbery was cleared, the spectacle made up for everything. In the garden, the trees and bushes were neatly cut and the small rose bushes separated the front drive from the garden in a semicircle. The driveway's stone covering was still yet to be put after the house got completed, but the garden could remain intact because the workers used only the service road running along the edge of the site. At least the park will look decent, if the workers will be performing acrobatics later on the scaffolding around the house. I was looking at the house from the wall running parallel to the road. Now it was even barer than before. The walls of the house were freed from the creepers, and the weeds skirting the base of the walls were gone too. That made the house look even bleaker, but I was happy because I knew it was going to radiate grandeur post-renovation soon.

The gardeners were very cheerful on their last day at work. I went to the brigade to thank them for their help, and I settled the bill.

"I'm glad you're in good spirits," I told the foreman.

"We are. You know, we were just kidding about who would be the next victim of the house..."

"Well yeah. I'm not worried, I'm neither a spy nor a black widow."

"Yes Madame. We just remembered the last incident and laughed at it."

"The latest one? Were you employed there in 1945, when the spy committed suicide?"

"No. The latest one. We talked about the janitor's son from the '80s."

I looked at the man questioningly. I don't remember reading about any death after the spy's suicide. Wasn't that enough for the house? How many more people could have died?

"What caretaker? Sorry, but I don't know anything about this period."

"You know ... after the war, the Japanese were given the castle for a while to use as an embassy. After that, it stood empty for a long time until it became a children's holiday home. Then there was a guardian in the castle. John Smith's parents and John himself for a while. The dumb petrol station attendant Johnny cheated on his wife with another girl from the village. When the wife found out, she committed suicide!"

My eyes widened and I just stared at what I heard. To this, the boss continued, confused:

"But I'm sure nothing like this can ever happen to you. I mean, your husband is a very decent man, so you are a decent couple ... and ..."

"Don't bother, I understand the joke." I tried to hide my fright behind a confused smile and quickly changed the subject, having paid the gardener. The workers continued to pack in embarrassed silence. After we finished settling the bill, I felt compelled to raise the subject again.

"You know, I'm an optimistic person. I'm sure nothing can happen to us that happened to these people in the past." I was trying to be convincing, but we both knew that these things had long gone beyond human will, and when it comes to this hose, no one could make such pronouncements for certain.

"Yes, ma'am," the boss said, "sure nothing will go wrong!"

At that moment, he looked into the distance behind me and tried to focus on a suspicious figure walking down the road. I turned to look at the phenomenon. The man was taking a photo every few meters with a camera in his hand. I apologized to the foreman and quickly ran to the stranger. He took a few pictures of me as I was approaching him with dirty hair and grubby gardening clothes.

"Welcome!" I said in a cold and measured voice.

"Good afternoon!" He replied in an ingratiating tone.

"You know you're taking photos in a private area?"

"Am I?"

"Indeed! And as such, I need to ask you to leave my property immediately."

"Oh! So I'm lucky that I get to meet the owner," he intoned, trying to save face, even though he appeared to be fully aware of the fact.

"I'm the owner all right, but you're not in luck, I can assure you! Why did you take pictures of the property?"

"I work for the local newspaper and for days I have seen movement in both the garden and the house. I thought it might be a good topic for the next issue."

"A good topic? Well. First of all, you are standing in a private area, trespassing, as I do not recall you asking for permission to enter. Secondly, you took the photos without asking, which is also illegal, so I must point out that if I see these photos in any newspaper, you can be sure that you and your newspaper will not get away with this without meeting legal action."

"My apologies..."

"No, sir, I'm sorry, but this is out of order. What on Earth were you thinking? Invading private property because it's "interesting"? You know, if you had contacted me via phone or come here and inquired about taking pictures first, I'd have been very happy to help. But as you have come like this, I have to ask you to leave immediately! Have a nice day! And don't forget the lawyers!" I yelled back over my shoulder on the way back to the house. "Silly scribblers," I laughed. "What was this man thinking? Ah, they have no style."

"We hope the workers will fence off the area as soon as possible!" said the gardeners' boss.

"I hope so, too! I'll talk to the supervisor as soon as possible to find out when it was planned for. Who knows when the next pack of hyenas are coming."

I said goodbye to the gardeners after also agreeing with them on the upkeep of the garden.

"Mr. Taylor!" I hurried to the construction manager.

"Yes, Madame?"

"Did you see the scribbler just now?"

"Yes, Madame."

"When are you going to put up the temporary fence around the site?"

"We'll do that soon. We will definitely start tomorrow or the day after tomorrow."

"That'll be very good! You know, I don't want the media to hold anyone up."

"There's another problem here, ma'am, not just journalists!"

"Oh, no! What's wrong?'

"You know, we've started preparations for the roof to be repaired and the facade to be scaffolding while the guys are cleaning out the basement. We found a narrow door there. We still don't know where it is leading because we couldn't open it and there were traces of masonry over an old doorway on one of the walls. It must have been very old. According to the plans it could be reopened so we did, but it would be nice if you would come down to see this too. Archaeologists are examining the objects now."

"What objects?"

"Come."

We were on our way to the cellar. I walked carefully over the wooden planks that had been laid for traffic on the uneven ground. They lit up the whole cellar with a very bright, reflector-like lamp. There was a shabby table beside one of the walls covered with a nylon sheet. The archaeologist handled the objects expertly.

"These were in the wooden box. Look!"

The archaeologist was holding the remnants of a fan. Its gilded wooden handle was filled with tiny patterns. Black silk ran in a semicircle, painted with beautiful floral patterns. It didn't look youthful, it was more like an object for a more mature lady. The next item was a chipped teapot, with worn patterns curling around on its side and the end of the spout broken. The inside was black as if something had dried up in it.

"This rifle here, ma'am, is over 100 years old, and so is this sword. I need to take these items to the lab for examination."

"Of course. Do what you need to. What kind of paper is that?"

"Medical report on the suicide of Eugene Nedeczky. It's from 1914."

"What? What is this paper doing here?"

"It seems as if someone had collected these items for some reason and hid them behind a bricked-up wall. Maybe so that they would not be found later. In that era, no one could receive a Catholic ceremonial burial if he had died by suicide. It would have been a great disgrace for the family to find out, so obviously they hid the case as much as they could."

"No secret treasures? Disappointing!" I joked about the situation, but the archaeologist replied strongly.

"None."

"All right, I think that's enough for me today. I'm going home." I turned to the construction manager. "I'll be at the hotel, if anything comes up, call me anytime."

"All right. Have a good rest, ma'am."

THE FAN

I got a fever by the evening. I was tired from the avalanche of information and the events of the day. I couldn't write anything, my head throbbed so much from what had happened. Depressed for weeks due to writer's block, and even the things I started ended up in the trash. I've only been keeping up the dream diary for months, but not even that attempt of mine is successful. It was so easy in my childhood, now I can't do lucid dreaming, even though I've done my best. So I took out the laptop and wrote a letter to the publisher. I am aware that I must deliver the script by the deadline stated in the contract. Still, I wrote to John to make him aware of my situation. Paul tried his best to lift as many burdens off my shoulders as he could.

"Let's go to Bad Füssing. We love that place and a couple of massages would do you a world of good."

"I can't. We can't go now. They found a lot of objects in the house, and I wonder why they might have been there. I had to throw out a journalist today. And the gardener's story was downright bloodcurdling."

"What kind of story?"

"Ah, you won't believe it," I sneered. "Someone killed themselves in 1980 as well. More specifically, the caretaker wife's because of jealousy. How surprising, huh? Hope you'll never get anything on the side, honey!" Paul laughed.

"No, honey. I love my wife, even if she gets upset about everything around her."

We cozied up in bed, and in the silence of the evening, my brain went into overdrive. Who and why bricked up that cavity in the wall? And why was it those objects in particular that they had gathered? Poor old man, he didn't leave his birthday to chance... And whose was that fan?

I'm standing in a makeshift salon. As if it were a century earlier. Alien furniture and an alien house. A woman is sitting on a sofa in a salon. She is reading a book. The salon door creaks and a fragile, pale girl comes in. Wringing her hands, she sits down on the couch next to the sofa.

"Mama! Tell me why do I have to do this?"

"Emma! This is just the way gentlefolk roll," replied the older lady in a voice that could not be opposed. "Wealth and family must be kept together! It has always worked like this. How do you think we could keep our rank and standard of living any other way? And women have this role to play. We have to care for our husbands, it is our duty to love and respect them, also to take care of our offspring. Your father is in financial trouble, and the family's fortune can only be preserved if you marry your father's brother."

The young girl's head bent down, and her mother continued in a softer voice.

"Eugene is a good man; you'll have a good life with him. He'll save us from disgrace. And you will do your duty for the family! And not a word more about this! All right?"

The elderly woman stood up, flushed her fan open with a single motion, and withdrew from the salon, indicating that the conversation was over.

She walked past me as if I wasn't there. But that fan! I was excited to see the fan. That was the fan the workers found! The fan was worn and tattered, but now it looks completely intact and new. What am I doing in this era? It was at that moment that I realized I was in a dream. I realized that I was dreaming, that is, anything I wanted could happen. The girl in the armchair began to cry. It was heart-rending to see. I wanted to go over to her, but when I started, everything fell apart ...

I can hear the sounds around me. Paul is rattling in the kitchen.

"Good morning, sunshine! You want coffee?" He asked, kissing my neck.

"Well… now I can't comfort the girl."

"What girl?"

"The girl I dreamed of, Emma. You know, the wife of the first owner of the house. I must have mentioned her already. She didn't like marriage. Her mother commanded her to marry her uncle."

"Ew, that's sooo…" Paul pulled a grimace.

"Yes, I think it's repulsive and causes a genetic mutation and all, but at that time it was normal among the nobility, you know. And imagine: I realized I was dreaming. I wanted to comfort her, but you woke me up," I said to him in a whining, sleepy voice.

"Oh, poor baby. I'm sorry! If I make you a coffee, will you forgive me?"

"You've got away with it this time, I'm not having your head taken off," I laughed.

THE VIEW

"We were lucky with this mild winter," Mr. Taylor began his report. – "My men could work through the winter without a break. The east and west wings on the front end are ready, and the attic room is fully finished too. And in the east wing, we fitted the museum hall as you requested."

"Are you finished with that too? Amazing! I never would have thought that they were working so fast, Mr. Taylor. Can I see it?" I smiled with glinting eyes.

"Sure, let's go," the construction manager agreed with a nod.

"Thank you for taking on the artwork of the museum too. I don't know what I would do without you."

"We will try to do our best, ma'am, as the customer requests. But since you know we weren't progressing as we usually do, but as you requested, the back of the house still needs work. We did not even enter the northwestern wing except when we cleaned up the debris at the beginning."

We stepped through the front door.

"Amazing design!" I exclaimed, looking at the door.

"We had it made by the best carpenter, ma'am, based on the picture you gave us."

"Long live that craftsman!" I looked at Mr. Taylor with a grateful smile.

We set off in the eastern corridor of the front. On the left, pictures of the house lined up one after another. I wanted visitors to see what the castle looked like. When it didn't have a door, as a year ago, and when it was in its full glory in the '70s and '80s. We entered the room. The glass cabinets stood on modest but stable racks in the center of the room. The objects we found in the wall cavity were all on display. On the walls of the room were portraits of the past owners, with a brief biography, or fragments about them that have been preserved throughout history beneath the pictures. There was no picture of Emma, only in my memory from when I dreamed of her. Deep down inside, I was sure she might have looked the way she did in my dream.

"I'll go up and look at the turret room!"

"All right. Just be careful in the construction area if I may ask!" The team manager called after me.

As I headed upstairs, I admired every part of the house under construction. Day by day, it is getting more beautiful as the workers worked on the interiors.

I admired the carpentry work of the spiral staircase. It was gorgeous with its upward curving, freshly varnished carved handrails. Last time we walked this way, we stumbled up a life-threatening rickety wooden staircase, and now I see a masterpiece winding under my hand. I opened the door and the new parquet floor sparkled in front of me. I took off my shoes so as not to carry even a speck of dust in and went silently to the window to admire the panorama.

The room is still empty, it's time to furnish it in my mind. The window frame has been beautifully restored with a high gloss, snow white lacquer. I ran my palm along the surface of the frame, and at that moment the colors disappeared from my eyes, everything became black and white. As if something had changed. I clasped the window frame with both hands and stared out of the window.

Not a soul anywhere. The asphalt road flanking the first half of our estate had disappeared. I don't see the Balaton sailboats in the harbor either. As I stared at Lake Balaton, its colors appeared and grew even stronger. Then, suddenly, the colors and the lights became more and more intense. Yes, that's it. I'm in my dream! I know I'm here. Otherwise, Lake Balaton wouldn't be so unnaturally blue. Nor would the color of the trees in the garden be so vivid. Like when we were trying to set the color on our television back in the 1980s. If we went over the limit, the colors got blurred along the outlines. Now I could try jumping or flying again, like when I was a kid. But I'm not at home now. This is not my home ground. I need to find out why I'm here, I thought to myself, in place of the neighboring houses, only unsightly agricultural fields. I stepped back from the window and found a young girl standing beside me. Startled, I backed away. She wore a long, white, creased nightgown. Her face was pale and tormented. She watched the panorama for a few seconds through the window, then turned and, walking around her bed, went over to her desk. She didn't look like a ghost or a harmful being.

She poured herself tea into a cup from a small decanter but it was as if she had poured water mixed with tar. She stared at the cup for a few more seconds in agony, then, with a decisive movement, she downed the lot. She looked at the window, not noticing me, as if I wasn't even there. She set off toward me, to the window but collapsed after two steps.

I jumped over to turn over the body on the ground and check its pulse. I don't know, it's a natural human reaction to want to help a defenseless person, but as I reached out, my hands ran through her body. Then I tried to grab her by the shoulder, but my hands hit the parquet. I didn't understand what was going on around me, but my nervousness mounted each minute. I was helpless. I had no idea how I could help this unknown woman. I knelt beside her and looked at her chest and the jugular on her neck. Her pulsating heartbeat gradually faded away under her skin and her chest no longer rose and fell. She was motionless and apparently, irrevocably dead.

I'd never seen a person die. "And what's this room?" I looked around frantically as she stopped moving. Beyond ancient furniture and in place of wallpaper, wooden ocher yellow panels on all walls, candles everywhere. Wash basin, clothes chest. I lowered my head and closed my eyes. I didn't understand what it was. My heart was racing because of the shock. By the time I reopened my eyes, everything was gone. I was back in my empty, newly renovated room. The colors are dull again, as they are in reality. I sat nervously, gasping for air for a few minutes, leaning against the wall. I was covered in sweat and my heart was still racing. Then, after a few minutes, the empty room became so strange and so quiet that I couldn't stay inside anymore. Slowly,

I got up from the ground and walked out of the room. Before I closed the door behind me, I looked back one last time, but saw only emptiness and the shadow of the window frame on the freshly varnished parquet floor.

I slowly walked down to find the construction manager.

"Are you all right, ma'am?" He asked, looking at my face anxiously.

"Yeah, I'm fine. I think I'm going home to rest now. Tell me, do you have any more business to do in the turret room?"

"No, ma'am. That room is finished."

"Then would you kindly lock it, and if I may ask, no one should enter it from now on."

"All right, ma'am. Are you satisfied with the job or do you have anything to be looked at again?"

"No, Mr. Taylor, no. It has come on beautifully... The view was perfect..."

THE BLACK POTION

Why didn't I think of helping her? Why couldn't I control the moment, so that she would not drink the shot? I should have recognized the fact that I can change my dreams. I must have failed because I did not control my emotions and I was too upset. Next time I need to be better prepared.

I was wearily pushing things about on the desk in my hotel room. My notes have grown into a messy little mound. I should rest, but the memories don't let me. Memories emerge from dreams. I can almost recall my dream when I'm awake. I can also call this progress.

That's it. I've found the article from the old newspaper. Thanks to the digitalized world, all newspapers will be scanned shortly. I lay down on the bed and started reading…

"Monday. It happened in Balatonederics this summer that Steven Papp, an old servant who worked on Eugene Nedeczky's estate, at the so-called Black Castle, fell in love with the widow of Carl Simon, Karolina Getri, a 58-year-old lady, but she was keener on younger guys. Dejected and desperate, Steven Papp murdered Karolina by stabbing her thirteen times one night after stalking her behind the ivy bushes. Dr. Endre Weisz, a young attorney who had never before worked on a case defending such a terrible crime, gave a well-rounded grand presentation. Of particular interest was the argument that it is not premeditation or a fit of passion that counts as aggravating or extenuating circumstance of a crime, but how lowly, or virtuous the criminal is, or what the state of mind, the root cause of a bad deed is. He mentions that this idea had already been raised in 1843 by Francis Deák and discussed by László Szalay, Pulszky and József Eötvös too, but for some reason it did not make it into our criminal codex, though it was adopted by foreigners and included in theirs. Prosecutor, Dr. Gerő Szász presiding juror, Vilmos Heinrich. Alexander Horváth head juror, Aurél Skóday, Joseph Siposs, judges, and Eugene Fülöp, notary. Steven Papp was sentenced to ten years."

Just ten years? Oh you cowboy, what have you done? Although journalists aren't exactly lost when it comes to juicy topics, this too might be as overblown and bizarre as my dreams. But what kind of relationship did he have with Emma? We know the servants did not really mingle with noble blood, well, men... but let's not go into that. Who knows what might have been going on...

The lurid world returned.

"Lock the door, Karolina," Emma said weakly, lying in her bed.

"Yes Madame."

Here's my cook, I thought, it's her I've been looking for. I'm dreaming again! Calm down, just playing head cinema, don't get too worked up about it."

As the door closed, Karolina hurried over to Emma's bed.

"Miss Emma," she pleaded "promise me you'll be healed." She knelt beside her bed.

"No! I do not want to. I no longer have the strength. You understand, don't you? This was not the life I dreamed of for myself. I can't pretend anymore. I can no longer bear to have my body humiliated."

"But he has never hurt you. Then why?" The maid asked desperately.

"I fulfilled my duty which the family expected of me. Now it's my turn. God forgive me for what I'm about to do."

"But what are you going to do, Miss Emma?"

"Listen carefully! You're not just a cook. You are my confidante and my only friend in my miserable life, so you have to do something for me."

"Anything! Ask for anything, my dear friend!" she said to Emma, kissing her hands.

"Make the black potion!"

"What??? No! Don't! My lady! I beg you, for God's sake! You can't do this!" Karolina protested.

"Yes, I can!" Emma snapped, summoning her last strength to show her determination. "Tomorrow night everyone will be at the ball. The doctor too. In the afternoon, when everyone is busy, you cook it and bring it to me in the turret room. Then you leave me alone. When my husband comes home, you come up to my room and clean up everything! Do you understand?

If you don't do it, I will dismiss you from your duties," Emma said. But they both knew this couldn't happen. "The doctor is hopeful, but I know I'm going to die. I no longer have the strength to suffer."

Karolina tried to suppress even her breath so that she would not break out in loud sobbing. Her tears poured silently as she squeezed Emma's hands in quiet desperation.

"By the time the doctor arrives, the poison will already be gone from my body. No one will find out you helped. You do it for me, right? If you love me, you will fulfill my wish and you will not let me suffer any more."

The maid nodded silently at her mistress's last request. She buried her face in the bedding and sobbed in pools.

"I'll do it, miss." The maid headed for the door, to which I intervened, crying out:

"What? You want to kill her just because she ordered you to?" in my desperation, I did not know what argument I could bring up. And what about the Christian spirit? You can't kill her!

Karolina turned halfway in the room:

"What did you say about Christianity?"

"Nothing, Carolina. I didn't say a word," the woman turned away from her maid.

"Hey, I'm here! I'm talking to you!" I waved my hands in front of her but she didn't notice. I became more and more agitated through frustration.

"Just because I heard... sorry." The maid went out. And the door closing seemed as loud as if someone had dropped a whole wardrobe beside me.

I woke up! My heart is pounding again. Why can't I control my emotions? Lucid dreaming will never work if I let my emotions rule me. And why is it morning? I just fell asleep a few minutes ago. Ah. I slept through the whole night in my day clothes.

CHAPTER 13

SHEYLA

I was wandering around in my hotel room with a stale pizza slice in my hand – which made me feel like I was cruising dangerously close to becoming a slob – when I heard a knock on the door. Who the hell could it be at the crack of dawn? I looked at the clock, which showed half past ten. Then I established I was right to get upset about the hour.

I opened the door.

Her chestnut brown hair was perfectly arranged on both sides, with the first strands sporting curls as usual. And her understated makeup lent even more majesty to her gray-blue eyes and lively face. Elegant, beige, knee-length dress, freshly ironed, making her look like she had just stepped out of a fashion magazine. Because of her perfect appearance – which is natural to her anyway – I felt light years of difference between myself and her.

"Hi Mom!"

"You are beautiful as always! Hi sweetie. What are you doing here? Um, did we talk about you coming? Come on in!" I said, sleepily.

"No, but I knew you'd be here!"

"What if I'm in Pest? Or at the construction site? Or if I am I hiking in the area?"

"Mooom!" she looked at me with a raised eyebrow and a sneer. "You and *hiking*? Don't make me laugh! When was the last time you went hiking with Paul?" her eyes burrowed into me.

"Well, it was… I don't really know." Before he left, we walked to the next village to the restaurant.

"Yeah, that was what, 600 meters perhaps. Congratulations!"

"Enough, kiddo, let's have a coffee instead." I stumbled toward the kitchen.

"Leave it, Mom. I'll make your coffee. Go take a shower and get yourself together instead. You look like a…" she trailed off in the middle of the sentence and smiled diplomatically, "well, you could use a shower."

"Thanks honey. Do you have anything else to say today?"

"I have. Where is Paul?"

"He went home to evaluate a project, and will come back soon. It's pretty hard for him to do this commuting."

"Poor thing. Anyway, I'm here to hang out today with you. You know, girly time together. On the way I saw placards saying that there would be an auction in the village. We could go there!"

I stood stiff with the towel in my hand.

"You and auctions? You know what they sell there?"

"Yes, old furniture. You like old furniture, don't you?"

"Yes, but you… it can give you the screaming ab-dabs, well, almost. Honey, when it comes to talking about furniture, your vocabulary consists of a right angle, a straight line, and the adjective *modern*."

"Yes, but," she began, confusedly, "I took on an extra subject at the university, and the dean said it wouldn't hurt to reinterpret the old styles. So are we going?"

I was trying to figure out the real reason, because I know my own daughter, and her newfound interest in the old style anything didn't seem credible much.

"Okay for me, but don't whine to me if you are bored halfway through."

"Hey, Mom! I'm all grown up!"

"Yes, I keep forgetting that." Sheyla looked askance at my skeptical expression, so she continued to explain.

"I'm doing my best to become an interior designer. You know, a career. This is important to me, I really like this topic. And you always said that you can be happy if you can do what you love to do. Well this is what I love! Anyway, we could go out to dinner somewhere afterwards and you could tell me how your new book is coming along."

"Well, it isn't. I haven't even started yet. I have no ideas at all!" I shouted out of the shower. "The editor will kill me if I don't submit a finished book in a few months. That'll be my credibility and the hefty checks out the window. So I'm starting to get a little tense about it."

"Then you might want to give yourself a kick up the proverbial, no?"

What a pleasant surprise, I thought to myself. My daughter has become a mature, serious woman.

We sat down in our seats in the local community center set up for the auction.

"This will take forever here," I whispered to Sheyla. "This is the fourth piece of furniture I don't like."

"No problem, Mom, we'll be done eventually. Oh, look, here's the next one. Buy this one!" she nudged my arm excitedly.

"*This*?" I looked grimly.

"Yes, this one! Well, do it for my sake. They will all be restored anyway, won't they? Well, go on, bid for it!"

I raised my arm:

"140 thousand..."

"Third time... Nobody? For 140,000 this beautiful sideboard is sold to the brown-haired lady on the far right."

"Here's the next one," Sheyla said again. "We need that too!"

I looked at her strangely. Why is she getting me to buy furniture she likes? And since when does she like old furniture?

"I didn't think you liked this style!"

"No, but this furniture suits you. Ah, trust me Mom, I'm the interior designer, not you... I'll know. Look, here's the catalog. I've circled what you still need to get."

"You're being weird today, you know?"

"Don't worry about it, just trust me. Then you can kill me for making you spend so much money. Okay?" she said with a smile.

"I won't kill you, you cost too much... you know, clothes, studies and stuff."

We both grinned at that.

In the evening, time at the restaurant passed quietly. The waiters were very nice and the food was excellent. We ordered the usual salmon with the usual brown sauce on top.

"So how are you coming along with the book, Mom?"

"Mostly know how. I have no idea what to write. The publisher said that the topic should be lucid dreaming."

"And? How are you with that?"

"At the very least I can't do it. I may not ever be able to. It was so easy in my childhood, but now... it is interesting that since the castle has been under renovation, I have always dreamed of its former occupants."

"What about them?"

"They all killed themselves!"

"Seriously? And you bought the house. Grand!" Sheyla looked shocked.

"I have. I squeezed out all the available information on the net, in the archives, here and there. It's quite a complex thing, but the point is that I think I dream about them because I've immersed myself in the topic."

"What if you wrote about that?"

"About the inhabitants of the castle? What would be interesting about writing about people who lived a hundred years ago? There is nothing interesting about them, except that they all committed suicide and almost all had the same first name," Sheyla laughed.

"Isn't that interesting? I think the story is weird enough. And what do you dream of?"

"I have dreamed of the first owner's wife and mother. They quarreled. Then, in another dream, she drank something that made her die. That was super realistic. Then the maid dream, when the wife ordered the maid to make some kind of brew."

"That's scary enough. And did you manage to steer your dream?"

"No, unfortunately, not yet. I recognize it if I am in my dream, and the last time my servant seems to have heard that I was yelling. But nothing more. I always wake up because I get so involved emotionally."

"I think it would be good for you to write this story. You're sure to get the most out of this one too. Try to get ready for your dreams in the evening while you are awake, before sleep. Discuss with yourself the idea that you will not become agitated, but only be present as an observer. Then maybe it will work. Don't try to just change it straight away, just be calm."

"Since when have *you* been a dream expert?" I laughed.

"You know, Mom, I too have been dreaming lately. You used to tell me a lot about how to differentiate and what to do. I think I followed your instructions well."

"Did you? I am pleased about that. And what do you dream of?"

"Just the future. I see my friends many times when we go somewhere or do something. And I always remember what was going on. Since then, my life has changed."

"Has it helped?"

"You don't know how much!"

My daughter gave me a poignant look. I thought if understanding her dreams helped her, she was on the right track. Although her gaze is so strange, there was more to it, as if she was trying to say something more. But she won't. She will when she wants to.

"Can we have another glass?"

"Of course!"

CHAPTER 14

DIARY DETAIL

Summer is about to begin.

I have the feeling that the house is coming to life, together with all its former residents. I was sitting on the sofa in the semi-furnished study. For now, there was only the rug in the middle of the room, my desk, and the sofa under the window. Around me were piles of boxes full of books. I'm waiting for the furniture, which, befitting a decent Library, will be a wall-to-wall carpet, built-in dark-stained hazelnut bookcase. My desk I got at the auction is beautiful. It was made of carved oak, between the two world wars. It's creaky and tottering, not that old yet.

I splayed out starfish-like on the couch and pulled a warm, soft blanket over myself. The rays of the sun stroked my tired face until I fell asleep.

I can clearly see I'm in a small temple. Up to the small altar, pews on two sides border the carpet running in the middle. Candles burning on the walls of the small room bathe the silence in twilight. A female figure is praying in front of the statue of Jesus. Me in church? I never go to church. It's clear that I'm dreaming! What did Sheyla say? Go ahead, calmly. As if I were an observer.

I slowly moved towards the female figure. Getting closer, I saw her face from the side; it was Emma. She prayed softly, muttering.

"Dear God, forgive my sin, which I will commit against my child and myself."

"What? Is she pregnant too?" I thought to myself, and knelt down beside her serenely, my hands clasped in prayer.

"Hello, Emma." She lifted her head and looked at me!

"How do you know me?" The young woman looked at me scared.

"Where from? Well... from the... vintage ball! Yes, I saw you there with your husband!"

"Where's your scarf, ma'am?" she asked, looking at me from head to toe.

"I left it on the car. I know it's inappropriate that I forgot, but you know, I don't think we have to cover ourselves up before God because he sees everything anyway. With or without a headscarf."

Emma pulled her shawl tighter around her shoulders as if she were afraid of something, but said nothing more, except prayer.

"You know, Emma. I understand people who want to end their own lives."

Emma looked at me again, annoyed and eager to leave, but I put my hand on hers.

"Listen to me, please! If you knew the time when God would be calling you himself, would you still do what you have planned?"

"Who are you?" her eyes betrayed fear and confusion.

"Believe me, I don't want to hurt you. I wish you well. I know you're mortally ill. Consumption is a serious matter. But please think over your plan. How would you like to leave? Do you want to be allowed into God's kingdom, or do you want to be condemned?"

The frustrated woman bowed her head and began to sob.

"No, I don't know what you're talking about."

"Yes you do. Give birth to your child, Emma, who is ordained of God's will, and then enter the kingdom of Heaven, pure as one would expect of a Christian soul. Gather what strength you have and fight to the last!"

Emma gave me a pained glance, then suddenly got up from the prayer bench and ran away. As I followed her with my eyes, the light that had penetrated through the open door was getting brighter, as if sunlight was intentionally flowing through the door. It's still getting brighter, and so are the candles. The flood of light is dazzling me…

I woke up. As I opened my eyes, the bright sunlight forced me to squint.

Oh my God! Success. I steered a whole conversation in my dream! It's unbelievable… But how was it? Yes. I walked in, talked, she cried, then ran away… I remember every moment. This is fantastic. I need to write it down in my dream journal right away. This may still come in handy in my book. Yes, I'm sure I'll write this story now!

Dream diary entry 142

"After many, many years, I have been able to consciously steer my dream again. I remained calm as Sheyla suggested. I think that was the step I needed to succeed. I am proud of myself for having struggled and got so far after so many unsuccessful attempts. And now I've finally succeeded. I talked to the person in my dream and even had a long conversation with her. This is a major achievement. That will be enough to get me started writing my book now."

It was a good day today. I think I'll invite Christie over for a visit. I picked up the phone and immediately called my dear "old" friend.

"Hi Christie!"

"Hi Lina! We haven't talked in a long while. What's new with you?"

"Oh, don't get me started. Our lives are a bit hectic lately, but we are getting on with things and making the place beautiful. The house will be ready soon. I just started moving in to the west wing on the front. I have a bathroom now and the kitchen is ready too. Well, okay. The carpenters are still at it assembling the Kitchen furniture, but in a few days and that's done too. So the house is echoing from the workers, but it's usable. The bedroom is still waiting, but I'll set that up with Paul."

"Oh yes? That's great to hear!"

"Mmhm, I'm very pleased too. Listen. I thought you could visit with us, your family of course, only if you have time and feel like it. Though the house is not ready yet, I'd be so happy to see you."

"Uh, that's a good idea, although I'm kinda snowed under too. The kids are going to perform a school play and I am making props. Now I'm hunting for a door for a scene, but I'll be able to solve it," Christie said optimistically.

"That sounds exciting."

"More like a small nervous breakdown, but the kids really enjoy it, so it's fun. Wait, I'll look at my calendar to see when I have half an afternoon free."

"Oh, you'll squeeze me in? That's very kind of you, thank you."

"Don't be fooled, I'm only going for the coffee!" she replied jokingly to my niceties.

"And how is your book coming along?" I inquired excitedly since a long time had passed, but I also knew that being a teacher, her life was not easy. At home, her own kids take up all her time, and she is a pretty active participant and organizer in school life, so it's really a mystery to me how she even has time for dance lessons to nourish her soul.

"What book?" she asked.

"Well, about the castle. When you were my first guest in the castle, you told me you were writing a book about this story. You know! So, how are you getting on with that?"

"I think you've mixed me up with one of your writer friends. I've never said I write. I wouldn't even have the time."

I got a lump in my throat, suddenly I couldn't speak. I slowly lowered myself on the couch in shock. I definitely remember her saying she was writing a book about this story. I even shook hands with her in a symbolic welcome to her as a colleague. Now she says she doesn't write anything. Something's awry. Now uncertain, I kept probing.

"But when we met in the house, that's what we talked about. Didn't you send me a bunch of material about the castle and its inhabitants that you explored? Didn't you say you had even been in the archives? There's a lot of..." I didn't finish the sentence because by now I was completely confused.

"Me? I certainly haven't. We met in the castle, yes, but I've never been to the archives, I don't even know where it is! Lina, have you been feeling okay anyway? You're being a bit weird with this topic. Are you sleeping enough? Christie asked, confused."

I did not understand the situation and formed my reply slowly, thoughtfully.

"Well… now you say it… not really. Maybe it's just because of fatigue. Oh, yes, I remembered talking to the local historian about this. Sorry, I've been a bit all over the place lately, but now I remember..." I saved the situation with a quick lie so that I wouldn't look any more stupid than I already felt at that moment. "So when are you coming over?" I changed the subject. "The archive room is ready, full of the old paraphernalia we found in the basement. And I can make a coffee too if I really need to."

"Next week, Saturday afternoon, I'm good if I shift my afternoon lesson to Sunday with the little guy I teach privately."

"Great! Then I'll see you on Saturday. I'm glad you can make it. It will be lovely for me too."

"And you could do with a break too by the looks of it. I'll be there around two okay?" Christie said cheerfully on the phone.

"Sure, perfect. Then at two on Saturday. Kisses."

"To you too."

I swear she said she was writing the book. Something's awry here! She even sent me the materials. I'll check it in my mail, I thought to myself after we hung up. I sat down at my desk, turned on my laptop and opened my mail. I typed the email address in the search engine: no results found! That's impossible, I thought. I grew nervous because I remembered that her first letter contained archived pictures of an old map of the house from the archived land registry documents. In her second letter, she sent the beginning of the book she had started. I even remember her lines, I think. But how was it? Time tears me apart, I feel like I was just… then it continues somehow… and the end is, "so I became the sixth orphan… or something like that. But I know. I also remember the lines! I didn't write this! I've put many stories on paper, many worlds spun in front of my eyes, with lots of stories and fictional characters. I know I can distinguish reality from fantasy. At least I think so. Suddenly, I picked up the phone and called Paul.

"Hi dear! Listen. I have a very important question. Do you have any free time now?" I pounced on Paul in agitation.

"Of course my treasure. Tell me, what happened? Are you in trouble?"

"Oh, it's nothing. Or rather... no, it's nothing. I wanted to ask you, remember when we bought the house and went down there first as the new owners?"

"Of course I remember. Was that some quiz question or what?" he laughed, but of course I was still wound up.

"No, just... And do you remember meeting Christie? You know, the teacher I talked to!"

"Of course I remember. She made more of an impression on you than me, but I remember, of course," he continued in a funny voice. "But why are you asking? Has something happened to her?"

"No, nothing. And you remember me telling you she was writing a book about the former residents of the house?"

Here Paul paused. As if he were hesitating, thinking.

"I don't remember anything like that. You spoke in Hungarian. You know I'm sharp, but not sharp enough to learn your mother tongue," he joked. I had no time for humor just then, so I continued to interrogate him intensely.

"Yes, but I told you in the car what we were talking about. I know it was boring to you because you didn't understand anything, but I told you all the topics. That she is a teacher and that she has two children and that she is writing a book about the house."

"You said she was a teacher and had two children. But I don't remember anything about her writing a book. What's gotten into you, my treasure? Aren't you the writer?"

"Yes I am. But I'm not the only one on earth," I answered in a testy voice.

"Seriously? I never would have thought of that!" Paul retorted mockingly.

"Okay, baby, this was all I wanted to ask you. So you're sure you don't remember anything like that."

"No, I still do not. But if that's all you wanted to hear, I'd rather be going now because I have to work."

"All right, honey. Talk to you later."

"Okay. Have a nice day, Sweetheart."

"To you too."

I sat on the couch tight as a spring with the phone in my hand. My mind was racing with thoughts I couldn't grasp. I stared at the snow-white walls of the semi-finished library room, trying to think through what had actually happened. Option one: I'm starting to imagine things, because of fatigue or stress, and my mind scrambles information and/or I'm hallucinating. In this case, I must urgently find a psychologist! That much is sure. Option two: If my mind is not tripping, then the fact that I remember something that no-one else does is inexplicable to me! This is crazy! I was there, and so was Christie. I remember the scene when she said she was writing a book. I also remember reading the book she'd started that night. I also remember the lines of the ditty!

Something has changed. Something is different now from how it was before!

I have to do something with myself because this is intolerable.

THE PAINTING

Christie is arriving in two days. By then, I'd like to furnish the parts of the house that the workers have finished with. They are still busy in the east wing, but half of the first floor is now ready to receive its first occupants.

I've started unpacking the new household appliances I bought in the morning. I remembered the first owner of the house, Eugene Nedeczky. What kind of man might he have been? Was he a good man or a tyrant? How did he end up cutting his own life short? Was it because of his political situation, or because he felt lonely without his wife, Emma? Or was it merely due to the pain and suffering of rheumatism that beleaguered him in his last years? In which room might he have shot himself in the head? It would be good to know because people do not like to stay in a room where someone had committed suicide. Yet, if I take that view, I'm in trouble, because Nedeczky wasn't the only one who had ended their own life here. It is even possible that there is no room in the house where no suicide has occurred. Ah, these Eugenes... And what could have been the first name of the Black Widow's lover, the well-borer? I bet he was a Eugene too. Anyway, back to our Eugene I – if he was in pain, why didn't he make use of some kind of medication for it? To my knowledge, opium was considered good medicine at the time. Tinctures were flavored with cinnamon or saffron. Why didn't he drink these then? Maybe even these were of no use anymore? I'll never know unless I see it in a dream. I have already had a "pleasant" chat with his wife at church. Even if I was a hundred and five years late with the conversation, I would still put some questions to him in my dream. For example, how can a deeply religious man commit suicide, if it was that at all?

Except for my dreams concerning the old dwellers of the house, I can say that I'm very good at setting direction. I love to fly in my dreams, especially nowadays over the beautiful Lake Balaton. The way the reeds border the coast is unforgettable. I remember the way the small shoals of fish formed rolling spheres in the water. Then they assumed a crescent- or an elongated baguette shape. The sense of freedom that I can savor in my dreams is fantastic. These flights always relax, soothe, and recharge me. I needed this experience too because whenever I have characters in my dreams, I come around as totally drained. I feel more tired after waking in the morning than I do when going to bed at night. Even so, my body is rested, so I don't physically need to sleep. It is an odd feeling to grow worn out through relaxing…

Another evening has come around. The dust stirred up by the workers during the day has already settled in the house. And I haven't been able to banish the wretched fate of sad old Eugene from my thoughts. In turns folding and unfolding the smallish print of his face in the palm of my hand, I tried to read from the features of his face what kind of person he might have been…

I'm standing in a room.

The oil lamps flicker faintly around the walls of the room, because the rays of the setting sun still bring enough light. Huge cassettes on the walls, decorated with a thin pastel stripe pattern running vertically on them. There is a wooden calendar on the left wall. In the vertical support beam, three horizontally inserted wooden slats. On the top one there are numbers from 1910 to 1920; this was inserted up to the 1914 mark. The beam intersected the middle slat at the mark of March, and the lowermost one at the number 12. So today is the big day! He wants to do it today!

The wooden furniture is all evidently fresh made. A huge row of open cupboards stretched along the longer wall, packed full of books, porcelain, and relics. A huge sofa in the corner with its two ends flanked by armchairs and a large round coffee table in front of it. Above the sofa, on the wall, I glimpsed a huge painting. It depicted a young woman. In front of her, a boy stands, and her hands resting on the child's shoulders. But the woman's features seemed so familiar. I've seen this woman somewhere before. Yes. She's Emma. But here she seems to be older. And who is this child? So she went ahead with having the baby after all? But that's impossible, because in reality she committed suicide. How interesting – I flow on and on with my dream as if I were deciding what was going to happen in it. Well indeed! In dreams it is always us who decides, of course, only once we can steer them. But what is she doing here in this picture, with more mature features and a child? Could she be a relative of hers? This cannot be reality. It's a dream again. Otherwise, why would I find myself here again in a 19th-century room?

The colors come alive as I take in the details of the room. Yes, I'm in my dream again. In the middle of the room there is a huge rug with a desk on it. This too, is in a brand new condition. As if someone had just had it made. On the desk leans an elderly, balding, gray-haired man. With his perfect outfit, he has already given himself away to me. His military uniform, crisp and pressed, evinces its wearer to be a man of honor. He lifts his quill to take ink from the black marble ink holder in front of him. He dips the quill in, then looks up at me and stiffens. His deep-set blue eyes are in stark contrast with his robust, bony features. His grey, full, bushy beard envelops his twirled moustache under his snub nose. He addresses me with a sudden quizzical frown:

"Who are you, lady?" He slowly lowered his quill onto the ink holder.

"Good afternoon, Mr. Nedeczky," I started in a friendly voice. "Perhaps your valet has forgotten to report my visit. I'm the village doctor's wife."

"That's quite impossible, for I know Mrs. Csapai and her husband very well indeed. They are old friends of mine. But you're not Mrs. Csapai. But who are you then?"

"I'm Mrs. Louis Burgundy. My husband and I have just moved to the village. He's also a doctor. The Reverend at Sunday Mass kindly recommended that I pay you a visit by way of an introduction. Unfortunately, my husband has taken his leave to Vonyarc for what seemed to be an urgent case, so I have had to come alone."

"This is unusual in the extreme Madame, but do take a seat. How may I be of service to you, Madame?"

I stepped a little closer to him and wondered how I could guide our conversation consciously. I find myself here, so let me try to make the best of it. I wanted to admonish him for his suicide anyway. Well, now is the brilliant occasion to do so. I looked at the painting again, then back at the man.

"Your dear family?"

"They are. They were my family!" he replied with muted passion in his voice.

"May I ask what has happened to your lovely wife?"

The old man leaned back in his armchair and sighed deeply.

"Shortly after the painting was finished, the Lord called both of them to himself. First his mother and then a few weeks later our child too. They both died of consumption."

"I'm terribly sorry to hear. When did they pass away?"

"In 1889. They didn't live to see the palace in its full splendor, though I had built it for them. But do tell me, what brings you to me, dear lady?"

"As I have mentioned to your highness, my husband is a doctor. And since the Reverend suggested that we might visit you, I would take it upon myself to recommend the services of my husband, a man of great learning. Should anything be ailing you". I didn't break character for a second. In fact, I got quite carried away in it.

"The dear Reverend. Yes," he said in a weary, jaded voice. "The dear Reverend sees everything, even things he perhaps shouldn't! He never gives up."

"What do you mean by that, sir?"

"Allow me to note, my lady, that this is a quite private matter. With all due respect to you, I do not believe it should concern you in the slightest!" he replied with piercing hostility in his eyes.

"Is that indeed so? Then do go ahead!" I pointed to the rifle on the table. "I would never prevail upon you to stop you doing something as important as ending your life. In fact, if you think it'd suit you better, I'll leave you to do what you have planned for today," I hissed in a cold, contemptuous voice.

"How do you know?" He asked, stunned.

"I took one look at you and saw it written all over you that you were about to throw away your life. I simply don't understand why?" My questioning look pressed for an immediate response from the grey-haired gentleman. He wavered; his face became one of a man undone, and he began to speak.

"The Reverend is aware of what I've been through to alleviate my pain. There is no mud bath in this or the surrounding counties that I haven't visited for a course of treatment. There is no herbal tincture on the earth that I have not applied. To my shame, I have already called a witch to help me, but she hasn't helped me either. I have no words for the pain that this rheumatic pain plagues me with. There is nothing else I can do…" he fell silent and looked hopelessly at his rifle laid across the end of his desk. Then he continued with indignation in his voice…

"If our Lord were so merciful, why would he take away everything I want to create? Everything I've started or whatever I liked he has taken away. I got married, our children were born, and the Lord took them. I set up a vineyard and sent me this plague, which destroyed everything I had created. I fought for the independence of my country, yet everyone gave up. We had to put the love of our homeland on a new footing to save it. We failed there too. We were in jail and it was only thanks to our uncle Deák that we were released."

Suddenly I remembered Francis Deák's lock of hair, which was so reverently preserved in the archives to this day. But my thoughts were interrupted by Eugene's violent soliloquy…

"I retired and quietly tried to be of service to the country as a Member of Parliament. Then came my brother's irresponsible, wasteful ways. He squandered his wealth, leaving many hungry women all around himself. I don't understand why I'm telling you this. You yourself are just a woman too. How could you ever understand the burden a man has to carry on his shoulders?" not pausing to hear an answer, he kept pouring his heart out…

"But he left them! God rest my poor good brother's soul, he might even be playing cards now, if God is merciful to him. That's why I married Emma. I had to save our family from disgrace and poverty. That's why I bought my brother's castle across the road, on the lakeside, and Emma's peachy young face... that innocent face, the way I saw her grow into a young lady... I fell hopelessly in love. But she never returned my love," he said desperately, pouring a cup of wine down his throat. "And now? Ma'am, tell me, what can your husband do to help me?" He looked at me with desperation and mockery in his eyes.

"You know, dear sir, over the long years I've seen many people in the care of my husband. Maybe none of them had pain as severe as yours. Suffering tends to distort people's virtues and have them accountable as failures. We see our actions in a worse light, even if they seemed to be the perfect decision at the time. Maybe that's why you shouldn't be so embittered. Where is the spirit that made you great? The noble soul that dictated to you how to protect your home and save your family.

You are a great man, Mr. Nedeczky. And what you have accomplished in your life is already more than what ordinary mortals do. These are your virtues that you should never forget.

The question is, how do you want to be remembered? Broken, as someone who has given up everything" I looked at the weapon on the table "or with your head held high, proudly following your uncle, Deák?"

The balding man stood up from the table. Slowly, he took the gun and shuffled to the commode near the wall. He lifted his gun and hung it on the wall. Then he said:

"I've never seen a woman state her case so freely and wisely. Women chatter a lot too, but you... You're not afraid of anyone if I see rightly. And smart too. I admire your husband for being able to handle you."

"Yes, this is my husband's merit. His open mind allowed my ideas to soar. The virtue of a woman does not begin and end with motherhood. We need to be strong to support our husband in difficult times. Maybe you should nourish your soul with your love for your wife. You're a warrior. Remain for posterity a strong, true Hungarian nobleman who fights to the death, who defeats everything until God summons him to Heaven. As dignified as you have been in your life, you must be to the end. It's the duty of a truly noble soul. Have you forgotten?"

The gray-haired man stared at me for awkwardly long minutes. In turns outraged that a woman dared to proselytize to him, and ashamed of himself for having forgotten what I'd said. He breathed hesitantly, as if not sure whether to continue this embarrassing conversation, but then he piped up. He shuffled back behind to his desk, then leaning on it, he looked at his wife's countenance hanging on the wall.

"I'll follow her… when God wishes me to!" he sighed forlornly as he looked at me again. "I'm going to see your husband one of these days," he reached out his hand, indicating that he considered the conversation finished.

I got what I came for, I thought to myself. And as I reached out to my hand to him, I deliberately wanted to put an end to my dream. So at the moment of the handshake, I looked into the man's eyes and said: "Lina, wake up!"

I woke with a start. The dim light of my little salt lamp infused the room with its yellowish light. The dream was as lifelike as can be. Uncertainty shot through me: was this reality? Or is reality me lying in bed? But it was no less real than me lying here now.

I stumbled into the kitchen for a glass of fruit tea and then slid back into bed to really try to regain my strength after the encounter with the gentleman and his painting.

SATURDAY

I finally got some rest. I was fumbling about in the kitchen as per usual in the morning. The two bottles of beer last night had worked a charm. I didn't dream of anything and found myself in the same position in the morning as I fell into bed in at night. I have a lot of preparation to do today as Christie is coming in the afternoon. In a few hours I will have unpacked all the kitchen utensils that are meant to represent the culinary equipment. Let's say the waffle maker was completely redundant at the moment, but I bought it anyway. Who knows when the urge to wolf down a waffle or three might waft into one's mind. Let's be on the safe side and get one!

It was half past two in the afternoon. I was done with the kitchen and even ran to the cake shop to fetch some snacks, but Christie was nowhere. I was hoping she was okay and on her way, just running late due to traffic. Still, my curiosity didn't let me rest, I grabbed my phone and searched for her number. I can't find her name in the list. This is very strange. Ah, what was her phone number? I remember the numbers were repeated and the last three were all 8s. I chanted the numbers I remembered, typed them in the phone, and called her. Yes, I clearly remember this phone number!

"Hi, Christie. So when will you get here?" I chirped, but at the other end a confused woman answered.

"Good Afternoon! Who am I speaking to?"

"This is Lina. Don't you know my voice?" I asked, smiling.

"Sorry, but I think you've called the wrong number!" Christie's voice became that of a friendly stranger's.

"You're pulling my leg! Didn't we agree that you'll be here by two? Where are you now? Are you stuck in traffic?"

"Sorry, but I don't know where exactly it is I should have been?" she continued, confusedly. It crossed my mind that this was getting beyond a joke and that something was wrong. Does she suffer from amnesia? Or what's wrong with her? Doesn't she want this friendship and is this how she'd like to get rid of me? That would be pretty childish considering our age.

"Christie! Listen! This is no longer a joke," I switched to a more serious tone. "We agreed that you come and visit me today. You know, I'm the friend you first met at the haunted castle by Lake Balaton," I added mockingly, sort of reminding her of my person. "We talked on the phone a week and a half ago, and you even said you were busy, but you'll squeeze me in. If it didn't work out, that's fine, I understand."

"Could you say your name again, please?"

"It's me, Lina!" I said, by now half an octave higher.

"Sorry, Lina, but I don't know you! I've been to Lake Balaton many times, but I've never visited any haunted castles, so I couldn't have met you!" Christie paused, waiting for confirmation.

I stood in the kitchen leaning back against the kitchen counter and felt my blood pressure plunge from desperation. I felt the power drain from my hands, and even my breath became heavy, choking. As I lowered my head to stare at the kitchen tiles, I noticed that I no longer felt the tea mug in my right hand. I started shaking and the mug slipped out of my hand. It smashed into bits by my feet, and the sound of the clatter yanked me back into the present moment. If I continue this conversation, it will almost count as harassment.

"I couldn't have met you!" I weakly repeated the last sentence of the alien Christie, which meant that our friendship did not exist!

"Are you all right, ma'am?" the stranger asked.

"You don't remember me," I said, swallowing my tears, and in the same breath, I hung up in silence.

I stumbled to the kitchen chair and sat down. Suddenly I began to feel dizzy. My mind couldn't take in the moment. I leaned slowly over the table and spread out my two hands palms down on the kitchen table to support myself. I had to feel solid matter under my hands, which at the moment seemed to be the only fixed point around me.

"Breathe, Lina. Breathe!" I chanted to myself. I need to get my blood pressure back up before I pass out on the kitchen tiles. After a few deep and slow breaths, I started thinking. How is it that Christie doesn't remember me when I do remember her? And the recent mix-up about her writing a book. Even Paul didn't remember it. Paul! I reached out to my phone again to find out what he would be saying.

"Hi, Paul!"

"Hi dear! How are you?"

"All right, honey." It crossed my mind that it would be good if I paid attention to what I said. Who knows what's going on around me now. In any case, it is reassuring that *he* at least remembers me. "Listen, I remembered what our first time here was like. You know, after we bought the house and came down to look around."

"Yes, I remember, the house was a derelict ruin."

"Yes," I tried to feign laughter, "and do you remember what happened there?"

"Of course I remember. What kind of a weird question is this?"

"Well, I was just feeling nostalgic and I remembered what it was like, and now I wonder, how you as a man, remember that beautiful day? You know, women and men always store memories in different ways."

"Yes, I know. Well, we drove a lot that day. There was dust and debris, and piles of bricks everywhere. But I was glad you were so enthusiastic about the house because it looks good now. You've put a lot of energy into it. Well, I won't forget that I had the feeling that the whole house was about to fall in on us."

Paul laughed.

"That's nice. I'm glad you remember that. But tell me! Did we meet someone there that day?" I asked, enunciating my words very carefully, because who knows how crazy he will think I am after this question.

"Meet someone? No. We didn't meet anyone there. Unless you mean the few unfortunate spiders you screamed at in the garden so loudly that they gave up the ghost right away," Paul laughed on the phone.

I caught myself not being surprised at his answer. I just accepted this next item on my list of inexplicable things.

"You're very funny, honey. Did you have a drink to make you so cheerful today?"

"No, I'm just glad we're done with the project. And the good news is I'm going home to you on Monday."

"That'll be very good! You know, I'm a little tired and I think I'll need you."

"Is something wrong, honey?"

"No, nothing serious," I changed the subject, "it would just be good if you were here already."

"I'll be there on Monday. And then we can go for a huge walk. Summer is coming anyway. It will be time for you to stretch your legs out there in Mother Nature."

"There's a huge garden for nature here, honey. That's more than enough for me."

"Yes, but it's different when we hike, you know. You can't sit in the house all day."

"Okay, okay. We can go if you really want."

"I'll see you on Monday, baby."

"All right, kisses, be good."

"Bye honey! Kisses."

As I sat in the kitchen, the silence whistled sharply in my ear. The birds' chirping in my ears quieted too; I just sat there. I sat, and my brain turned off. I glanced at the bowls on the round kitchen table full of chocolate cookies. Sugar is definitely going to do my low blood pressure good, so I started gnawing on a chocolate cookie. After the third one, I felt my body recover and realized what chaos reigned in my head that I needed to fix. And as if – as always – I was trying to untangle the knotted-up headset cord, I began summing up the situation.

Ever since we bought the house, our lives have become a bit hectic. I'm behind with things all the time and my work suffers too. There's nothing wrong with that. I'm in control of the situation, it happens to everyone. My first inexplicable memory, to which I have no evidence, is that Christie is not writing a book. The documents disappeared as if she had never sent them. And Paul doesn't remember Christie writing a book either. I'm the only one who remembers. I cannot blame this on my chaotic eating habits, nor on doing too little exercise to take care of my health. Then I might have some kind of a memory problem. That day I dreamed about Emma in the temple. I talked to her and then there was a problem with Christie. Could it be that exercising lucid dreaming will interfere with memory? It could even happen, as after a lot of practice, the dream imagery is almost lifelike. If I didn't know how my life was going on in reality, I'd be sure to confuse memories. Could it be that events in my dreams are changing the present? But this is nonsense. Even the presumption is pompous and big-headed. I'm ridiculous for having such thoughts at all. At the same time, my imagination is so pathologically untethered that I cannot exclude this possibility either. Perhaps I should be careful about this because

I might quickly find myself wearing a pretty little straight-jacket and escorted by a nurse or two in white. Still, the idea of finding proof of my crazy assumption won't leave me rest.

I spent the entire afternoon wrapped in a little summer blanket, hunched in the garden chair. I just stared at the garden and retraced every step until the sun went down. The soothing tea blend with the cleansing nettle leaves was of not much use either. I was hoping beyond hope for a miracle, one that would perhaps liberate me from my crazy situation, but none came. By the evening, I calmed down, and decided to try and prove to myself that I was not out of my mind. I need a simple memory that justifies me, and with which – if it can really happen – I would not radically change my current life. Whatever happens, only I will be responsible.

Returning from my evening walk – which I only went on out of sheer fright, in case my health was in trouble – I showered, headed to bed and began to search for my old memories. I was looking for something that was only mine that left a mark and that I can check now.

THE IRON

The morning sunlight violently tried to break through the heavy blue curtain at my window. It's morning and I feel as if I'd been shaking my booty all night in a nightclub. I closed my eyes again and tried to recall what I had dreamed of. I was in a childhood memory. Mom taught me to iron because she always went to the office wearing ironed clothes. Her blouses and skirts always lined up starched and sharp in her closet, and I was trying to imitate the perfect goddess my mother embodied. I'm ironing her skirt, getting pretty good at it now. The colors got blurred again and the black grip of the iron grew larger in my hand along with the lemon yellow hue of the summer skirt. With my right hand, I wanted to pull the skirt forward on the ironing board, but the nose of the iron in my left hand almost burned my arm. Then I suddenly snatched up the iron and put it down. I was very agitated in my dream. But, wait! That was the moment when I actually burned my arm, the memory of which I still carry on the inside of my arm.

Suddenly I sat up in bed and got my right hand out from under the blanket, searching frantically for the childhood scar, but it had disappeared. It's not there. I jumped out of bed and ran to the living room to look at my arm in the light by the window. I don't have it now either! It's disappeared!

I collapsed on the living room couch and looked around nervously.

What if someone found out? If anyone realizes what's happening to me. We've seen enough agent movies where people are indiscriminately killed. Or worse, they get experimented on. What is different is never average. What is different is always terrifying. Not comprehensible. Not ordinary. That's why people are afraid of it.

I think I'm scared of myself too! I mustn't dream any more. What if I accidentally can't control my dream? What if I do something bad and hurt someone? What if you accidentally hurt yourself and throw the present out of kilter!

Fear enveloped me. What tremendous superpower is this I possess? What can I do without people becoming aware of it?

The awareness triggered a severe headache and something began to tickle my nose. I rubbed it and as I took my hand away, I noticed that it was covered in blood.

God, now this as well! can't wait for Paul to come home. Should I tell him? No! That's out of the question. I couldn't prove it, because if anything changes, he won't remember it. I can't tell anyone. And from now on, I'm paying close attention to what I'm saying and to whom.

THE OLD

Paul arrived and everything seemed easier, as if by magic. I felt safe with him, although this did not have any effect on the inexplicable events. I didn't tell him what had happened to me. Until I figure out what's going on, I can't even give it credit in my own mind. I have to do it again. I can't reconcile the memories in my head. There are now two different sets of memories of several events. I remember burning my arm in my childhood, and I remember how the movement changed in my dream. I know I've met Christie, she can't be the figment of my imagination. It's very strange that everything related to her has disappeared. All the emails she's sent and her phone number from my contact list. Even though I remember her phone number. That's the only fact I can hold onto. You can't randomly make up a phone number and call it. The only evidence I have of what happened is only in my memories.

All the websites that refer to the "haunted" and "cursed" castle of Lake Balaton have disappeared from the Internet. No video, no photo galleries, and nothing about the suicide of the first owner, just a simple obituary. The obituary is from 1917, which is interesting because he originally died in 1914. But now I'm not sure of anything.

I remember the maid and the name of the murderer too. I searched for the man's name again in a Hungarian archive database. Does that mean it didn't happen? Well, I remember it. I need one more piece of evidence. In fact, more. Lucid dreaming is almost routine for me now. And anyway, so many violent people have died violent deaths in the infinity of time. Why should I not change it and help them leave the world of the living in a dignified way? Even if it doesn't matter to them. I fell asleep again to find Steven, the shepherd.

I was standing on the side of the dusty road. I turned around to see where I was. My eye caught the castle right away. I was amazed how beautiful the building was in its original state. The magnificently carved stone figurines were real masterpieces, glittering white along the edge of the balcony. I'm dreaming again! After all, I never could have seen the original house, built almost 130 years ago. So my first job was to find the shepherd. So I set off for the house. As I got there, I immediately assumed the role of the "local doctor's wife" and went over to Karolina, who was working in the vegetable garden.

"Good afternoon!" I said reservedly so that she would notice me there.

"Welcome, Madame! Can I help you?" she wiped her soiled hands into her apron, which was worn and smeared anyway.

"Yes, I'm looking for the shepherd."

"Steven? What business have you got with him?" she asked impudently.

"That's nothing to do with you, maid," I replied tersely, because all of a sudden I could not think of any reason.

To this, she huffily turned back to the vegetable patch and grunted back over her shoulder:

"He's in the back in the stables."

"Thank you!" I finished the exchange.

As I passed the house, the stench wafted into my nose. "I'm in the right place," I thought. A man in gray raggedy pants was working in one of the paddocks. His shirt may have been last white when it was made, and its cleanliness left something to be desired too.

"Good day to you, shepherd!" my voice jolted him out of his daze; he cast around nervously to see who could be addressing him. Then when he saw me, his tensed-up shoulders dropped and his posture slackened.

"Good afternoon, Madame!" he leaned on the pitchfork and fixed me with a questioning look.

"My husband is a local doctor," I began with the usual line.

"You don't look like Mrs. Csapai."

"No, I'm Mrs. Burgundy."

"Did my master complain about me?" he shrugged nervously, still staring at me with his deep-set brown eyes.

With such a nervous disposition, it's no wonder he killed the maid, I thought to myself.

"No, calm down. We've just moved into town. My husband and the Reverend agreed to visit everyone in the village. And if you have any concerns, complaints, feel free to contact him! We live in the house with the turret roof opposite the church."

"Since when are servants welcome there? I thought it depended on the goodwill of our master whether to call a doctor to their servants or not. How would we pay for the doctor, dear lady?"

"Look, Steven! That's your name, isn't it?"

He nodded curiously, waiting for an answer.

"My husband doesn't distinguish between people who want to be healed. Beyond fifty, sometimes our heads hurt because of fatigue, our backs ache, and I could go on. You don't have to be on your deathbed to see a doctor, and get medicine if you are tired."

"Well. Sometimes my back does hurt, that much is true. And I'm starting to feel that I can't keep up with my duties around the house by myself. And that woman there makes me mad from morning till night..."

"The maid?" I smiled.

"Yeah. The old wench is always teasing me, you know? Like the other day, she went down to the village with the neighbor's maid, Julie. The cheek! She does it one more time and..." he raised his hand as if ready to slap someone. "Well, that's what makes my head hurt, ma'am."

"I can understand that. Do you know that little plant with the yellow petals? Do you know the one that gives a purplish red liquid when you crush it? St. John's Wort."

"Yes, ma'am, I know which one you mean. I sometimes pick it for the master for his rheumatism."

"Great! Well! Get two more of those every day. Tell the maid to make you tea from those two every night for six weeks. But only pick the short-stemmed ones!" I raised my finger for emphasis.

"All right, ma'am," he said quietly now, smiling, still leaning on his pitchfork.

"You're a strong, hardworking man. Don't let tiny things spoil your days. Your master is already over seventy. He needs a good, reliable worker like you."

This was my goal. The shepherd stood up straight, as if he felt his own presence more important now, something the estate could not function without.

"Well, you might be right about that," he looked at me cheerfully. "If you don't mind, I'll have to get back to work because not even grass will grow without me here."

"All right. Have a good day, shepherd."

We finished the conversation jovially, and as I turned to leave the stable, I saw the face of a gorgeous horse staring at me with its huge brown eyes. Slowly I walked over to her, raising my left hand to caress her huge nose. As I approached her cheek, she gently tucked her nose into my palm. Then I said, "Lina, wake up!"

Something tickled my face again as I awoke. I had a nosebleed again.

Ignoring that, I grabbed my laptop instead of coffee to look for anything about the shepherd. I typed the keywords into the digital database just like before, but this time found nothing – the old articles I'd seen before were gone. No matches! This is again proof of my theory that my dreams are changing the present. But how is this possible?

I went to the local doctor, the real one, in the early afternoon for any insight into this, but he just said my blood pressure was a bit high, and I needed to rest more. And my coffee habit! I must switch to tea. Well, I thought nothing had changed in medicine in a hundred years. At most, humans are being poisoned by more artificial chemicals than before. I can count myself lucky he didn't give me a prescription.

Paul and I went down to the fair. All kinds of homemade sausages, pickles, bakery products were on sale there. We were only able to inch forward in the undulating crowd. The scents sneakily seeped into my nose and completely disoriented me; forgetting where we were going in the fair, my feet began to unconsciously follow one of the scents.

We stopped by an old stallholder and I admired the smoked goods with awestruck reverence in my eyes.

"Good afternoon!" I started the conversation with the head-scarf-wearing woman who was pushing 80.

"Good Afternoon! What can I give you?"

"I want that little smoked knuckle on the far end. That one there looks fresh! "I eyed up the small, reddish knuckle flirtatiously.

"Yes; no doubt of it. A good choice, ma'am! " the lady said. "Do you mind me asking if you are the folk who moved into the beautiful house along the way?"

"The beautiful house?" I blinked in surprise at the old woman.

"The one opposite the old inn, not far from the Africa Museum."

I admired the mysteries of rural life. Here, news has always spread faster than the speed of light.

"Yes, ours is the 'beautiful house', I said, "but how do you know?"

"Ginger told me. The doctor's wife said so. You know, she's my neighbor."

Splendid, I thought as I watched the nosy nattering woman, I'm sure the whole village knows us, if nowhere else, from hearsay. Pushing for further rumors, I kept probing.

"And why did you say 'the beautiful house'?"

"Oh, well, because that's been its name since I can remember. That's what the whole village calls it. It got its name after its first owner. He was said to have lived to a beautiful age. They say he lived to a hundred. And his shepherd went with him everywhere. When Mr. Nedeczky couldn't even walk... oh yes, I remember, he was called Nedeczky! Anyway, he always took his master everywhere in his carriage. They say he was parading in black livery in the carriage beside the old man."

"And how did he die?"

"Which one?"

"Both of them! Let's say..." I grinned.

"Well, it was straightforward. They were old!" replied the woman with ease.

Well, that's weird again. I looked at Paul in confusion because I knew it would be completely hopeless to explain why I felt like an utter fool again. The story of the house is completely different from what I remember.

"And there was never any scandal in that house?" – I kept asking.

"Scandal? Well, yes there was! The black widow. She didn't deserve that nice house. The village was also angry with her. She was a dirty, no good example of a woman and the way she treated her husband – she waved dismissively – the woman was scandalous, you know."

"What was the scandal?"

"Well, she was unfaithful, to which her husband committed suicide. Terrible. Then she cheated on her lover with a third. That one killed himself too. He hanged himself in the barn. But the third one, He avenged the first two. He well and truly milked the widow out of her fortune, then left her behind in her disgrace. The hag ended up selling the house too."

"Very interesting. Do you know of anyone else who died there? Maybe some cook or something."

"Cook?" she laughed. "Cooks are not murdered in decent houses!"

"Thanks for the quick history lesson. Really nice of you to let me know."

"Now that you've moved in," she smiled, "it doesn't hurt to know. You know how it is!" She gestured with her weathered, wrinkly hands, then folded them again to continue wringing them.

"I wish you all the best."

"Have a good day!"

As Paul and I turned away from the stand and we threw ourselves into the swirling crowd to continue the yummy hunt, my phone vibrated. I got it out of my pocket, and saw John's name on the display.

"Oh no!"

"Who is it?" Paul asked.

"The editor," I pulled a grimace because I'd known ahead of time that I was going to be in trouble because my deadline for the book had expired that week. My stomach became a knot; how was I going to explain this situation now? Then, coy as a coyote when he met Riding Hood, I took the call.

"Hi John, lovely of you to call."

"Hi. I am glad to hear you too. I'd like to know how the book is coming along. Your manuscript should have arrived in the office this week!"

"Wow, time flies, doesn't it? Damn. You know, I've been making great headway lately and I'm almost done, but unfortunately," – I started to slow my voice down – "not completely."

On the other side of the line, my words fell into thick silence, which is never ideal in the midst of an awkward conversation, so I pressed on: "But relax, only the last chapter is missing and I'll be done with it soon. Just give me three weeks."

"Look, Lina, I know it's hard to write a book to a deadline, but if this is so problematic for you, then we can arrange payment from the next copy-money, and forego having a binding contract."

"No no!" I exclaimed, scared. "I can do it. I just lost track of time a little. Just give me three weeks. You know what? Two. I'll send the manuscript within two weeks."

"Ten days. Get it to me by next Friday if possible. That I can just about explain to the company, but no more."

"Oh, thank you, John! Thank you for being so understanding. I'll be finished with the script by Friday."

"Okay, I'm waiting for it. As fast as you can, please!" – John said goodbye, and as I did so too, the line went dead in an instant.

Paul stroked my arm as he saw me cave in under the weight of my own ineptitude.

"Sooo, weekend getaway postponed, I take it?"

"Uhum. I have ten days to finish the book, which is impossible by the way, unless I hook up a coffee jug intravenously into my arm. Or I could get some speed somewhere!" a gibbering wreck replied from inside my skull.

"You can do it, relax," he embraced me. "We'll stroll home and by the time we get there you'll have a clear head. You'll take a shower at home, I'll make you coffee, and make some food, and you'll sit down, gather your thoughts and tackle to the end of the story. The point is, don't worry about anything else. I'm managing the household. Just focus on your job. All right?"

I squeezed Paul tight. My heart brimmed with a sense of gratitude and love for having such a caring husband. My rock in my haphazard world...

THE BLACK WIDOW

I sat at the desk with my jaw clenched and feet tapping. There are two more. I have to save them. Until then, I can't concentrate on writing either, because they're the foundation of my book. How could I finish my book this way? I could even come up with a story out of thin air, but that would not be a credible story for me.

I plunged again into the dark underbelly of the Internet in search for the "third cheater". In the March 1, 1935 issue of the Hungarian National Gazette, I did indeed find the answer to many things.

"It's a matter about adultery committed by a multi-skilled man. Dr. Louis Knight Vass, a forensic judge, today presided over the case of Adorján Káli Nagy, who was committed for trial on several charges of fraud and embezzlement. The tall, elegant man was led by a prison guard to today's hearing. When questioned about his personal circumstances, the judge pointed out that he had variously unlawfully pretended to be a landowner, a farmer and a seaman. The accused presents various documents to prove his allegations... Knight Vass then presented the prosecution's indictment. According to this, in 1929 he became acquainted with the widow of Dr. Eugene Vág, introducing himself as a retired sea captain, and claiming that he had a monthly pension of 900 pengoes. He also told the widow that he had a $ 100,000 claim due from the United States. Deceiving her with all of this, he married her and cheated her out of 10,000 pengoes. He is accused of buying his wife a 16,000-pengo carriage for the wedding, but deceived her into signing a bill of exchange for the same amount and spent the money he had thus gained. According to the prosecutor's office, from Futura he embezzled 3,000 pengoes, promised Mrs. Franz Keszthelyi marriage and cheated her out of 1,500 pengoes. He also deceived a woman by promising her employment her as a cabin attendant aboard his ship and extorted 300 pengoes from her on the pretext of needing a security deposit. The prosecution charged Káli Nagy with other minor offences too. The accused did not plead guilty... Later he came to Budapest with 50,000 lires and met the widowed Mrs. Vág, whose estate he wanted to rent. According to his statement, it is not true that he would have lied to the woman to gain unfair advantage. The fact is, he bought expensive jewellery for his wife, worked for his wife for a year and a half, and spent almost all of his money on converting and furnishing his wife›s villa in Balatonederics. When he was left without any money, his wife threw him out... He borrowed 3,000 pengoes from Futura with his wife›s permission. According to his account, his wife treated him very roughly in the last period of their cohabitation and this completely ruined his mental balance..."

Gosh! What a scandal this was at that time! I laughed at the thought. I imagine the whole village rumbling at the news.

Especially because there was such a scandal in the "beautiful house". The maids and servants arranged meetings in the market to keep everyone up to date with developments on a daily basis. They took a little away, and added a little on. Oh my God, what stories could have been circulating in the market?

The following articles describe the wife's infidelity from 1928, which led to her husband to committing suicide. Poor Mr. Vág, what could he have gone through? And here's the next part: "... after the well driller became the new lord of the house, the black widow ignored him and went on to seduce a third man. Therefore, the well driller, like his predecessor – also due to a broken heart – threw his life away..." After a brief search, I also found a document in which in 1941 the woman wanted to enroll her son in squire school. Boys over the age of 14 who met the requirements of the squire school were allowed to apply for entry there.

This is scandalous. The husband committed suicide, the well driller committed suicide, and the third man tried to make her destitute. But who is the child's father? With this density of traffic, perhaps even the woman herself did not know, being the harlot she was. Here is another source, according to which the lover had assumed paternity, but the woman denied him everything and, not caring about the moral standards of the age, continued her decadent lifestyle.

I have to change the past so that the unfortunate woman does not ruin so many people's lives, and she herself does not suffer such a fate. I need to visit the black widow!

Paul took care of everything around the house, and I heard him clacking the plates in the kitchen at four in the afternoon.

I stretched my limbs and headed out to see what he was doing. I shuffled across the living room. Crossing the kitchen threshold, I walked into the scent of my favorite soup.

"Hello, sweety!" he said.

"Ugh."

"I thought you could take a break. You have been sitting in front of the screen from morning to night for days. You started writing at dawn today. When again? At five o'clock? I don't even understand how you remember what you write without coffee!" He laughed at my professional neglect. "So I thought we'd eat a big bowl of soup and have something to drink," he looked at the Rosé wine on the table. Then he came closer to hug me. "I also thought I could give you a massage afterwards."

"Pleeeze don't let me stop you," I whispered. "But now I can't, I have to save two more people."

"Pardon?" I do not understand what you mean.

I suddenly woke up to what I had said. I mustn't say anything, that's for sure.

"Forget it. Only the characters in the book."

"Yeah, I see. The characters can wait while you relax."

He started kissing my neck to convince me of the need for a joint activity.

It was a pleasant afternoon. The wonderfully laid out table, the early dinner and Paul's attentiveness distracted me from the deadline. We'd only made it through half of the wine, but he was already fetching the next bottle with a grin and the air of benign despot. I felt tension drain from my body as a result of the wine and my thoughts kind of followed suit. Well, why not? One more glass won't hurt. History can wait, if that's how things have been so far, one more day doesn't matter.

We talked all afternoon when my darling came over to me after the last glass of wine, took my hand and pulled me naughtily towards the bathroom. I know this look of his. The look that smolders in every man's eyes when he wants to woo his lady and lovingly let her know who the master of the house is...

The next morning, I woke up with in a daze, yet the effects of alcohol had worn off. Immediately, I was wondering if I had dreamed of anything. I do remember Paul smothering me with his love until dawn. Maybe that's why I'm so tired that I didn't dream of anything.

Coffee mug in my hand, I pigeon-toed down to the study to continue my work where, exceptionally I found all the documents in place. I drew the huge blackout curtains apart, then sat down in front of the screen and started to "conjure" the last scenes into my book.

THE VÁGS

I'm standing by the lake. The last rays of sunset have painted the surface of Lake Balaton a muddled rusty yellow. The reeds had already coalesced into dark, indiscernible patches along the coast. The primordial darkness of twilight surrounded me, and the color of the lake turned a deceptively fiery red. So I'm in my dream again. I have to find the woman, I thought to myself, and I turned to see where I was.

The turret of the house stood unmistakably across the road. I got to the house in a hurry. A man was sitting on a bench in front of the castle. His hunched posture, together with his bowed head and his disheveled suit made him look broken. Like someone who's been sitting there all day hungry, thirsty, in a daze. I walked towards him tentatively. He lifted his head and stared at me blankly, as if he had not grasped that someone was approaching him at all.

At this moment I heard the sound of footsteps reverberating on the cobblestones from behind the house, to which we both looked over. A creature bursting with vitality emerged and proceeded toward the car in Charleston steps. She was wearing an emerald-green, boat-neck sequined dress that was tight at the waist and barely covered her knees. The wispy veil of her little black hat half-covered her face. Black silk gloves covered her entire arms; between her forefinger and middle finger she balanced a tapering cigarette holder with a lit cigarette in it. Her cheeks, bursting with health, were framed by her short, black, straight, gelled hair. Fiery red lipstick highlighted her lips, and her blue, kohl-rimmed eyes sized up all around her sharply.

Reaching the car door, she looked at me, and then at her husband. Despite his beseeching gaze, she indifferently took a drag on her cigarette, then sat in the car and drove off.

By the time I got to the man, our eyes had met.

"Good afternoon!" I began the conversation in a sympathetic voice.

"Good afternoon!" he replied with apathy and resignation.

"Is the lady your wife?"

To this, he lowered his head and stared at the garden in front of him.

"Yes, but not for much longer. She wants a divorce."

The man sat there as if he had been utterly destroyed. It was evident he was not in possession of his faculties. The world around him had receded into oblivion, for he even forgot to introduce himself.

"How about you? Don't you want to divorce?"

"I have no hope left. I'd die without her if she left me. Didn't you see how beautiful she was? How breezy, lively? And me, I'm just a boring lawyer. I carry papers around, I am tending to others' troubles and problems. While she… enjoys life."

"Why don't you do it together?"

"She forbade me to go with her. She said that women of the world no longer need a male escort. Didn't you see how short her dress was? Unacceptable. If they find out in the office, I'll be even more of a standing joke than I already am."

The man was so inconsolable that I felt sorry for him. I felt the desolation at the destruction of his love. I could almost see the fragments of his shattered faith in his marriage all around. A broken man was sitting on the bench beside me and suddenly I didn't know what to say to him. I couldn't reach him by trying to talk sense to him, he'd gone way beyond that. Any talk would be illogical in the world around him, and in fact, it wouldn't matter to him anyway, so I decided to be completely honest with him.

"Do you know why I came, Mr. Vág?"

"No," he looked at me blankly, as if he hadn't even realized he was talking to a stranger. Staring at the flowers, I started:

"Actually, I came to talk to your wife, but since she looked like she was in a hurry, I'm left with you as my last resort. I'll tell you what's going to happen. If you continue like this, you will arrive at a decision to throw away your life. Because your wife has another suitor, he will take your place, but she will not respect that person either, just like she doesn't respect you. By then your wife will be pregnant and give birth to her lover's child. Then, not sparing her lover, she'll look for yet another new suitor, to which he will respond in the same way as you are planning to now and commit suicide. Then, on the pretext of the third man's messy romantic background, she'll throw him out too."

The man listened to my story in silence, but did not react. He continued to stare at the rose bushes, as if he had not understood anything.

"Do you hear what I say, Mr. Vág?" I looked at his face from the side, but he was still rigidly staring ahead. Eventually, an answer fell from his lips.

"Yes. I hear you."

"You must do something!" I raised my voice, slowly enunciating my message. "Stop your wife! Tell her this can't go on! Do you understand me, Mr. Vág?"

"Yes, I do," came the reply.

A sense of hopelessness came over me. There was about as much life in the man as in the rose bush he was looking at. I might as well have been speaking to the wall of the house. That would have made as much sense as what I was doing. I decided to give up. Looking through the front yard of the castle, then staring at the gate of the estate in the distance, I said out loud, "Lina, wake up!"

I opened my eyes. It was still late at night and my body was still and cozy but the depressing feeling that accompanied me in my dream had not gone away. What a lame dream it was, I thought, it was going to change nothing. I didn't think the man even grasped what I'd explained to him. Better to try again another night.

Chapter 19

POSTFACE

I'll have time to send it to the proofreader and editor before sending it to John for translation. I corrected the last scenes in my manuscript on Thursday afternoon, and, having re-read my lines, I decided I liked what I'd written:

"Jennine was winding her way down the interminable corridor. Grasping her husband's arm, she limped on between the green-painted walls, to which she remained oblivious. She was not aware of reality, let alone where she was in it. She lifted her head for a moment, looked at her husband and mumbled with tears in her eyes, "I know that everything has changed! I know everything has changed!" Her husband gently pulled her near and all he could reply was, "Yes, baby. I'm here with you. Everything is going to be fine. I'll never leave you alone." With these words, he escorted her to a small, closed-off ward in the hospital, wiping Jennine's lips dry again and again as he did so. The shots of tranquillizers and mood stabilisers had worked. They'd turned the once lively, cheerful woman into a retarded, nodding houseplant. As David sat her down on her bed, she glanced at him again. With her pupils dilated enough to house a galaxy in each, she turned to the only man who could return

157

her faith that she might not have gone completely bonkers: "Do you believe me?"

I think I've whipped up a great story for John. They will be lapping up the dream hunter woman who went off the rails. The deranged darling. She ought not have told everyone her screwy story about her changing the past, then she would have had a chance to be free. Well, this could happen to me too if I don't keep on my toes. That's why I'm not going to tell anyone what's happened to me.

John's letter arrived on Saturday. He thanked me for sending the script by the deadline.

Paul and I were cracking open one of our favorite Villány rosés in the middle of the living room. We were about to raise our glasses for a toast, to celebrate me getting ready with the material in time, when we heard the sound of heels on the stairs.

"Mom, Paul! A voice echoed down the stairwell."

"Sheyla!" I told Paul. "She didn't even say she was coming."

"Hello!" Sheyla switched to German.

We always spoke in German when Paul was with us. It is quite uncomfortable to be in a gathering when you do not understand the conversation between the people you love and are close to you. Thus it became an international language.

"Surprise!" My daughter smiled and hugged each of us in turn.

"How come you're here?" I asked. "Why didn't you call, I'd have got us snacks."

"No need, Mom, I'm a big girl now. I thought we should celebrate because your book is finished. I see I've arrived on time!"

"I'm very glad you've surprised me. But how did you know I'd finished with my book?" I looked at her wide-eyed as she dropped her bag into the corner of one of the large sofas and sank into the cushion beside it like someone who's finally returned home.

"Oh, I was guessing. Or rather…" she paused "…I was hoping you would be ready by now."

I didn't believe her. My daughter is so weird lately, too serious and too grown up. Or is it just me who refuses to see how time flies and believe that everyone is acting their age. I scrutinized her for the answer, but her poker face obscured everything.

"Alright darling. Want a glass?" I nodded at the Rosé bottle.

"Of course. I'm sleeping here at home today and I don't want to drive anymore today. So, fill it up, Mom!" she said with a smile.

I was already taking the glass off the bar shelf.

"What title did you end up settling on for your book?"

"Variations on History."

"And? What was the end of the story?" Sheyla asked.

"Ah. Poor Jennine got banged up in the nuthouse. Her husband escorted her wherever she went."

"Oh, poor thing," she and Paul opined in unison with a Cheshire grin.

"I had to finish it that way. It can't have a happy ending, none the least because I've decided it's going to have a sequel!"

Paul and Sheyla perked up and intoned:

"You don't saaay! Congratulations! What made you decide on the sequel? And what about the woman? Is she gonna come out of the looney bin? Yes, yes. She coming out?" The questions rained on me. With my best mysterious fake-bitch face on, I said:

"A writer will never tell you what they'll write until they do!"

That did it. They unleashed themselves on poor me.

"Well, well," Sheyla laughed, "that'll teach you not to give me that great writer pose here!"

"Yes!" pitched in Paul. "Excuse me, when you got stuck, you whined to me, *Oh my God, how will I keep going? Paul, you gotta help me!* Pff, I won't help you anymore!" He folded his arms, turned his head away, smiling, as he played the victim.

"Ah. You don't even know how glad I am to have finished it. I was tying myself in knots as to how to wind the story up, but in the end I got my mind unfolded and did it. I think this is going to be a good book."

"I'm sure," Sheyla said. "Meanwhile, have you finished the back garden, Mom?" she changed the subject.

"Sure, it's been two weeks already! But you haven't even seen it. Will you take a look?"

"Sure, let's go."

"Go on, girls. In the meantime, I'm gonna fix lunch," Paul said.

"Salad with fish, isn't it?" Sheyla asked with a grin.

We exchanged a knowing look by way of an answer.

"Salmon, please!" Sheyla told Paul.

"Okay, I'll take care of it," he said, and with that, he poured another cup for himself. "As you're heading there anyway, bring two more bottles from the cellar, please."

"So what gives? What's up lately?" my daughter turned to me.

"All is well, honey."

"You don't say. When I talked to Paul last time, he said that you have had nosebleeds pretty often lately."

"Yes, but I think it's just because of lot of stress."

"Mom, stress does not give you nosebleeds. When did it all start?"

We strolled over to the front garden bench by the greenhouse and sat down clutching a bottle of pink each. I unscrewed the cap on my bottle, took a swig, and began pensively:

"I have had nosebleeds since... since..." I faltered because I was afraid my daughter would think I'd lost it.

"Ever since you started lucid dreaming!" she finished my sentence for me completely matter-of-factly. My eyes widened and I looked at her questioningly. How does she know? And why is it so natural for her?

"Now you're going to ask how I know. True?"

I had no idea what to say to her, just stared ahead silently.

"I'll tell you a story, Mom. It's about an old man, let's just call him Eugene. Our hero was living in an unhappy marriage because the woman he loved, who was not altogether coincidentally his wife, was constantly cheating on him, so our unfortunate man committed suicide. So, later on, the woman sought a new victim to satisfy her, and teamed up with the man she had been cheating with. But not even this satisfied her, she cheated on her lover with a third one, so the second lover also committed suicide. You know the story, right?"

"Of course. You're talking about one of the owners of the castle who lived here. When did you research what had happened here?"

By way of an answer, Sheyla took out her phone and handed it to me, where I saw an old article downloaded from a database.

"The catastrophe of the decade! Eugene Vág, a lawyer from Pest, gave a testimony in prison. A man of good social standing had lost control over his faculties due to insanity. He pleaded guilty before the jury to the murder of his wife's lover in a moment of passion in his villa in Balatonederics, and then, to her murder too as he'd feared that his wife would keep on cheating! The brutal double murder is aggravated by the fact that she was pregnant. The night after his confession, Mr. Vág hanged himself in his prison cell. The prosecution has named Eugene Vág the most brutal serial killer of the decade."

"I do not understand this. What is this?"

"That's what you screwed up, Mom!" my daughter said admonishingly.

If this is the reality here, then is this article the new reality? Is this the end? Is this the effect of my conversation with Eugene Vág in my dream? Jesus, what have I done. I made the past even more tragic with this. But if that's the reality now, then...

"Do you remember what really happened?" My heart started racing and I gasped for breath.

"I do. Are you surprised? You taught me to dream, Mom. More specifically the basics of it, and I improved on it over time." Sheyla took my hand. "I know you're lost and have a lot of questions, but first of all, calm down, I know you're not crazy. Your nose is bleeding because you've changed the story many times."

"Because I've changed it a lot? What makes you think this? How do you know these things?"

"I just do, and that's that. The bottom line is that you have done quite a good job without any help, all things considered. Congratulations, Mom," she said matter-of-factly. "But now you have to stop dreaming to recover and have nosebleeds again. You need to concentrate so you don't dream of anyone! You have to learn this too. Otherwise you see what kind of disasters you can cause. You don't want me to go into detail about what could happen if you dreamed of your own childhood and screwed something up? You know everything has an impact on the present!"

Sheyla paused for a moment and that moment was just enough for more questions to arise in my mind. The sun was scorching my shoulders more and more each minute. This wasn't making me feel well. And the scent of the garden flowers didn't soothe me anymore either. I felt stupid and irresponsible. And full of myself for imagining that I could help everyone. And now

I was confronted with the fact that I can destroy as well as build outcomes. Sheyla squeezed my hand and continued:

"Mom, you were very good. I'm proud of you. Don't worry about Vág now. We'll fix the mistake. Now, think about how to learn not to dream! I know what it is like when you get into the swing of things in everyday life and have a winning streak. Things get better and better. You can teleport yourself faster and faster wherever you want. And, in the end, you see and control every detail. First you are proud of yourself for being able to do so. Then complacency sets in because you think you can do anything. Which is true. In a simple lucid dream, you do what you want. You are where you want to be and do whatever you want. It's safe and free. There is no responsibility. But not in the dreams we dream! You and I do it completely differently. This is no longer simple lucid dreaming, you noticed that too. As you woke up from a dream, everything had changed. We must be very cautious. Paul's not like us, Mom. You can't tell him because he wouldn't understand. You can't even tell anyone else, otherwise you'll end up like Jennine in your book."

I looked into my daughter's eyes. There was no poker face now. Now I saw the deathly serious gaze of an adult, without a trace of her childhood or teenage girly self.

"Do you know who Christie was?" I looked at her questioningly, and as I waited for the answer, time seemed to stretch on into infinity. For me, this answer was the most important thing to have it confirmed to myself that I was not in fact crazy.

"Of course I remember her. You talked about her on the phone six months ago."

"But she doesn't remember me anymore. She didn't recognize me on the phone after I dreamed of the first owner of the house last time."

"You surprised, Mom? You changed the past! This castle was only interesting and exciting as long as it had a past of everyone committing suicide here. Of course all the stupid tourists flocked here to see the country's only infamous castle. And you ended up picking it, because you were also a stupid tourist here with Paul," she laughed, taking the edge off my mournful mood. "Now that it has become a 'beautiful house', no one in the country knows of it. Only the locals and the monuments office."

"How can I make Christie remember me again?"

"That? Know how. Maybe you will meet her later," she said mysteriously.

I just stared into the middle distance and tried to grasp this new information. So my daughter knows it too. I mean, she understands, being just like me. Then I started to weep because of the tension.

"I thought I'd gone mad," I said, to which my daughter turned and hugged me, swapping roles with me, as it were. It is as if she was the mother who soothes her desperate daughter with her tight embrace. Then she looked me in the eye again and smiled reassuringly:

"I know. That's why I came! But I'm starving now, Mom. Paul must be ready with lunch by now. You know, he can whip up any kind of meal in twenty minutes. Come on, let's go eat. Try to get yourself together and calm down. You know, the way you taught me to. We never despair, and always find a resolution."

Again, I unscrewed the bottle cap and gulped down a much larger mouthful of pink than before. Better than pills from the pharmacy.

Sheyla stayed with me for three full days. She never stays that long, or at the most when we go somewhere on vacation. She's always busy or hanging out with friends. Until now, I thought she was living the life of ordinary young people. But knowing she has these abilities, how does she live her everyday life? Could it be that not even I know my own daughter anymore? She's still young. When we are young, we change so quickly and so do things around us. How much control does she have over her own life? In any case, we had a lot of fun during family time together. I escorted her to the car.

"This I've held back on some. Until you've grasped all the information I gave you."

She placed a sealed envelope into my hand, which she pulled out of the glove compartment of the car.

"What is this?"

"An invitation."

"How many more are there? People like us, I mean."

"A few. In the meantime, don't dream of anything!" she commanded me in a very stern voice.

"I'll be there," I said as we squeezed each other tight. She doesn't even protest any more. When she was a teenager, she hated being squeezed and hugged like a rag doll. Now she's grown up and learned how to give love with an embrace.

She got in the car and started the engine. Before leaving, she smiled at me and said:

"I know you'll be there!"

CREATORS' GROUP

I'm past my third coffee this morning. It's been a few weeks since my daughter gave me the invitation. Weirdly, I've been looking forward to it so far. But this morning, I'm just busy with finding the perfect dress for the occasion. I'm a typical woman. Standing in front of the mirror and deciding about wearing my mauve summer dress or the ecru costume I bought for our 5th anniversary last year. Five years ago, that's when it all started. My real career and my whole life. I don't even know who I was before then.

"Lina!" Paul shouted from the kitchen, and I back:

"Yeah?"

"You should be making tracks!"

"Yeah I know."

I heard his footsteps approaching the wardrobe in the bedroom.

"These darned clothes. They get smaller every year! And always in the summer! It's dreadful."

"Yes, it is," Paul smiled, hugging me from behind and stroking my belly.

"Could you stroke one of my sexier body parts? Say, my butt or thighs?"

"All your body parts are sexy. You should just do a little more walking, Sweetheart," he covered my neck with kisses, then nuzzled it with his face. "Do you remember how lucky you were to find this house? The beautiful house! Good thing you found that ad in town while we were here, otherwise we'd never have found our house!"

Suddenly I didn't know what to say. I just stared at him saucer-eyed, and I wondered how to keep my expression in check so as not to give myself away. What kind of ad is he talking about when we first glimpsed the house together from the car on the road? Doesn't he remember it? Or maybe he remembers something else? God, how could that have happened in his memory? I hope nothing else has changed in our life! Hope he will still recognize me tomorrow!

A sense of loss struck me, so I turned around and put my arms around him. I squeezed him tight to feel reality in the present moment. If this was our last hug ever, I shouldn't miss it by any means.

"I have to go soon," I muttered into his neck while biting my mouth inside, lest I let fear get the better of me and make me cry.

"All right. Will you take coffee in a thermos?"

"That will be a lifesaver, yes," I said with a forced smile.

I shook my head after Paul left the room to return to the present. I don't like either dress. The dark brown lacy cocktail dress will suffice. I'll put on a coat and a low-key scarf with it. Want to avoid standing out. I can fully understand women in their dress dilemmas. Although I'm the type who doesn't vacillate much. I opened the closet, and picked the one that appeals to me. Normally I don't think about this for hours. How long have I been standing here now? I should check my emails. John must have written about the book already. And Christie? What might be the matter with her? Sheyla said maybe I'll meet her. Oh, I mustn't forget my socks I wear for driving. I haven't even watered the flowers yet. Oh, Lina, you're starting to fall apart. Stay focused! Get dressed and go!

I parked in front of the conference center shown on the invitation. I put on my high heels and shoved my driving socks in the glove box. This is where the party is meant to be. Actually, I reckoned it was too much effort to dress up for five or ten people, but decided to keep things neat anyway. Sheyla always looks like she's just stepped out of a catalogue in her freshly pressed clothes. Wish I knew where she gets it from.

I was standing in front of the revolving door of a huge glass building. After I went in, the porter guided me towards the meeting room. I looked at the bar in the lobby and thought I'd rather sit down for a cocktail, but it's not on the agenda right now. A man in a suit was standing in front of a big door. I stopped a fair distance from him and started reading the triangular board on the ground.

"Welcome to the 20th Creators' Group Conference.

Programs:

From 10 am Monthly evaluation of private projects

From 11 am Group reports

12-12: 30 am Break, smorgasbord buffet

From 12:30 pm Further ethics training for moderators

From 1 pm Further training of the Memory Group

From 2 pm Further training for Directors

At 3 pm Welcoming of new members.

Entry by invitation only. "

"It will be an interesting day," I thought to myself. "I think I'll check in at the suited gorilla." I approached the heavy-set man with the gentle smile. He held a list in his hand. I gave him the invitation, which he looked at carefully, and with a wide grin on his face, he opened the door of the hall to me.

I'd been expecting a lot of various things at the entrance, but not the need for a five-hundred-seat hall for this "party". An enormous semicircular hall with four pillars, around the walls muted lighting, which fell on the beige striped wallpaper. The inlaid floor was divided by a red runner that stretched all the way to the stage. The hall was almost full of people. Suited men and women in chamber suits were mingling inside. But this medley of people still seemed somehow different. They weren't stiff and formal with each other. Their body language gave away a lot about them, the way small conversation circles closed in on themselves. They were direct and friendly. I wanted to admire the huge chandelier that descended into the middle of the room too, but at that moment a young man came up to me. A suit lends every man a distinguished appearance, but I was still more intrigued by his facial features. A blond, blue-eyed, friendly-looking but tight-faced young man looked at me. All in all, he was a pleasant sight to behold, even if much younger than me.

"Welcome, Lina, if I may call you by your first name. I'm Peter," he offered his hand for a handshake.

"Good to meet you!" I shook his hand and looked at him, curious as to what he might want from me.

"I'd like to congratulate you on your new book. It is fantastic what you've achieved in your career as a writer."

"That's very nice of you to say, but I'm still waiting for feedback from the publisher."

"Oh, sorry, so you don't know it yet."

I looked at the man, confounded as to why he was congratulating me on something I didn't even know about. I looked past the man's arm and saw my daughter approaching us.

"Hi Mom!" She hugged me then stepped back and put her arm into the man's. "I see you've met."

"No, not really yet, but the young man has already congratulated me on my book."

Sheyla looked at Peter.

"I told you to keep your mouth shut," she muttered to him.

"Okay, but I wanted to be the first one."

"All right," she cleared her throat, then continued after a deep breath. "Mom, let me introduce my boyfriend, Peter."

"Oh I see!" Now I understand the introduction. "I'm very glad to meet you." I looked at my daughter. "But why didn't you come home to introduce your partner, Sweetheart?"

"It wasn't a good time last time. I rather wanted to be alone with you. And I thought today would be a good time to make introductions."

"You have surprised me for sure. Does your dad already know?"

"Not yet, but we'll see him next week. But we should go now, Mom."

"Where? Don't we sit down? This is where the show is, right?"

"Not for you, Mom, come on. Let's go upstairs and I'll tell you everything."

We walked down the stairs and I wondered why I couldn't sit with the other people.

What is this mystery all about? What is all this toing and froing?

"Here we are," Sheyla opened one side of the French door, "let's sit down by the window."

The three of us sat comfortably in a quiet, smallish meeting room. There were only the three of us inside, and the lights were redundant, as the window looked to the huge showroom, so the light that filtered in was enough for us to see each other.

"Well," my daughter began in a grave voice, "I'm sorry I took so long, but now is the time to talk. Obviously, our last conversation raised more questions in your mind, which I will all answer now. I didn't tell you everything last time because it would have been a lot of info for you all at once. Not just for you, it would be too much for anyone. So don't worry about that. But before I get started, you have to promise that you will forget for a moment that we are mother and daughter and that you will not interrupt, just listen to me patiently."

"All right. You couldn't be any more mysterious if you tried, so tell me."

Peter pulled out a tablet from the inside pocket of his suit and handed it to my daughter, then she looked for something on it and gave it to me.

"Read this, please!"

"What is this?"

Sheyla nodded in the direction of the tablet in response, indicating where I ought to look.

It was an article from an archived version of an old newspaper:

"Eugene Vág was appointed president of the Hungarian Bar Association. He was welcomed at the inauguration ceremony… he moved to Budapest with his family, where he began to hold the office of President."

"Who did this?" I looked at Sheyla, shocked. "Is this THE Mr. Vág? There are many Vágs who…"

"Yes it is!" she chirped. "Read the next one," she said, shifting the windows where some archived material was scanned in.

"My dear friend! I and my family have cheated death, and left everything behind. We had no choice. Please take care of the manor until I return home from America... Eugene Marich, September 24, 1947"

"He defected? But, in theory, he committed suicide."

"He didn't. Or rather he did, but now that there has been a change in the wind, we consider the Nedeczky project complete."

"What do you mean the Nedeczky project is complete? And who's completed it? What's all this? Kiddo! Get talking or I'll keel over with a stroke. I do not understand anything. Why are there multiple versions of a memory? And why not one? What do you have to do with this whole incomprehensible mess?"

"Chill, Mom. Do you see that crowd down there?" she pointed down to the huge hall where the show was well underway.

"Yes I do."

"He's the president," she pointed again at the stage, where a man in a suit was standing. "And the many people down there are the Creators' group. This is a non-ordinary conference for those who want to learn to fly in their dream or who are looking for a relationship with their higher self. This is the hardcore here. The crowd is made up of four groups. One is the Directors Team, where you belong too. You can dream into the past and change events that can have very serious consequences. Think about why I told you to learn not to dream.

Then there are the Moderators. I think you may have realized that I and of course the rest of the group are dreaming of the future. This is completely different and more complicated. Because the future is constantly changing because of the decisions we make in the present, we have a pretty hard time doing it. However, we are indispensable in being able to keep tabs on things changed in the present or the past and to react in time to the new alternative present.

The most important ones are the Researchers. With each "operation" we change something, and so does the information. Data from the Internet, archives, whether paper-based or electronically archived, disappear. So they are our memory bank. Special people with a photographic memory who have the job of learning all the information they can. As there have been several "operations" in the past, the present is changing. So when they go back to the past in their dreams, their job is to search the archives. Of course, ordinary people notice none of this. For them, the current world is always the original one. Only we know how things have changed. That's why researchers are needed.

They need incredible concentration to extend the time of a dream or event as much as possible. This way, they are able to stay in one focused dream at night, unlike us or ordinary people who have 3-4 dreams a night."

As I listened to Sheila, my body shuddered at the realization of what all this meant. Peter coughed subtly, signaling that he would like to take the floor.

"The Nedeczky and the Thief projects started because Sheyla said at a meeting a few months ago that you had begun practicing lucid dreaming. The Thief project was needed to get you started with the Nedeczky project step by step. Do you remember what they found in the cellar gathered together?"

"They were on display in the museum room for visitors."

"That's right!" Peter continued. "When your nose started to bleed, we knew you had crossed the standard line, so we asked one of the researchers to work with us on the project. Usually 3-4 people cooperate on a project, so our researcher looked at the original memories and also reported any changes as soon as you made them. We were prepared for the possibility of failure because you were not aware of the rules, so a "Clarifier" from the fourth group already made arrangements as to where to step in and effect corrections. Which was needed, after all, because before clearing, Mr. Vág had become a serial killer, remember that, right?"

I sighed heavily.

"Yeah, I think I managed to mess things up there."

"No problem, we've resolved the issue. But overall, as the history and data of the entire house have changed, the perception of the house in the recent past and the present is completely different. At the moment, nobody knows the house, only the locals, to whom it has not made any difference, as there are many derelict castles in Hungary, and this is just one of many. Nobody likes or knows it. And the state it was in before your dreams, when it had damage done by the local lads, no longer exists. This meant that since it was not in such a dilapidated condition, its purchase price was much higher when you bought it."

"How come I don't remember it?"

"Probably because you are still in the practice phase. Each group goes through three levels of learning. You are now at the first level of study. You have just learned to change the past, and you must also learn how to recall the new memories and information relating to everything you have changed. As the memories double, the corresponding area responsible for the storage of memories in your cortex increases. That's why your nose started to bleed. You made several changes in a short time, and your brain was unable to keep up. So the point is, when you go home, check your current bank transfers and take out your contract. Memories of how much the house actually cost and how it looked without damage will come up."

"But if it cost more, where did I get the money?"

"You're sharp, Mom, I see. Did you think you got so rich and famous off your own bat? I'm sorry, don't get me wrong, you really do write excellent books, but in order to generate that kind of revenue, we also had to involve the San Francisco team to get them behind the advertising. That's what made your books so famous."

"But then... isn't all this my merit after all? That way I'll never know what kind of writer I am."

"It doesn't matter now. You cannot irresponsibly keep readjusting the past whenever you feel like it. Every change has very grave consequences, which can be both good and bad. You need the ability to consider what you may end up causing in the present or future with your decisions. Do you have any idea how difficult it was to organize the auction? The running around Peter had to do to find out where the damned furniture was? And then to organize the whole thing. Invite people who don't want to buy that particular piece of furniture. I nearly died as we sat through the auction. Yes, Mom, you guessed it, I don't like old furniture, but we were forced to do it because when I dreamed of the future, I saw all the furniture in the house."

"Fine. I guess I didn't grasp anything. I reckon it's either me who needs a shrink or it's you..." I looked at them in complete confusion. I simply could not fit into my mind what they were saying. My whole body started to tremble, and my mind turned off all thoughts. I stared down at the crowd. I am not special! And I'm not the only one either. There is a whole army of people with similar abilities. Even more, they are united. And unity is also power...

"Come on," Sheyla said, "let's go down and drink something at the bar before you collapse. Then we'll sit down and listen to the show. And in the afternoon you have to be on stage with the rest of the rookies. Look! Those in the front row are going through the same thing as you today..."